ALSO BY JANICE GALLOWAY

The Trick Is to Keep Breathing

BLOOD

BLOOD

Janice Galloway

RANDOM HOUSE
NEW YORK

Library of Congress Cataloging-in-Publication Data

Galloway, Janice.
Blood / Janice Galloway.—1st. ed.
p.   cm.
ISBN 0-679-40594-1
1. Working-class women—Scotland—Fiction.   I. Title.
PR6057.A397B57   1991   823'.914—dc20   91-50135

Manufactured in the United States of America

2 4 6 8 9 7 5 3

FIRST AMERICAN EDITION

This book was set in 11/13.5 Linotron Bembo.

Book design by Carole Lowenstein

To Peter K.

Acknowledgments

Grateful acknowledgments are due to the following, where stories appeared:

Aktivismus, Arbeit, BBC Scotland Short Stories, Behind the Lines (Third Eye Centre), *Chapman, The Common Thread* (Mandarin), *Edinburgh Review, Glasgow Herald, Kultur, Margin, New Statesman & Society, New Writing Scotland 6, New Writing Scotland 7, Northern Lights* (Unwin Hyman), *Original Prints 2* (Polygon), *Original Prints 3* (Polygon), *Radical Scotland, Sex and the City* (Serpent's Tail), *Streets of Gold* (Mainstream), *West Coast Magazine*

In the United States:

Conjunctions 17, The New Gothic: A Collection of Contemporary Gothic Fiction (Random House)

Contents

BLOOD

Blood

He put his knee up on her chest getting ready to pull, tilting
the pliers. Sorry, he said. Sorry. She couldn't see his face.
The pores on the backs of his fingers sprouted hairs, single
black wires curling onto the bleached skin of the wrist, the
veins showing through. She saw an artery move under the
surface as he slackened the grip momentarily, catching his
breath; his cheeks a kind of mauve color, twisting at something inside her mouth. The bones in his hand were bruising
her lip. And that sound of the gum tugging back from what
he was doing, the jaw creaking. Her jaw. If you closed your
eyes it made you feel dizzy, imagining it, and this through
the four jags of anesthetic, that needle as big as a power
drill. Better to keep her eyes open, trying to focus past the
blur of knuckles to the cracked ceiling. She was trying to
see a pattern, make the lines into something she could recognize, when her mouth started to do something she hadn't
given it permission for. A kind of suction. There was a
moment of nothing while he steadied his hand, as if she had
only imagined the give. She heard herself swallow and stop
breathing. Then her spine lifting, arching from the seat, the
gum parting with a sound like uprooting potatoes, a cool-
ness in her mouth and he was holding something up in the

metal clamp; great bloody lump of it, white trying to surface through the red. He was pleased.

There you go eh? Never seen one like that before. The root of the problem ha ha.

All his fillings showed when he laughed, holding the thing out, wanting her to look. Blood made a pool under her tongue, lapping at the back of her throat and she had to keep the head back instead. Her lips were too numb to trust: it would have run down the front of her blazer.

Rinse, he said. Cough and spit.

When she sat up he was holding the tooth out on a tissue, roots like a yellow clawhammer at the end, one point wrapping the other.

See the twist? Unusual to see something like that. Little twist in the roots.

Like a deformed parsnip. And there was a bit of flesh, a piece of gum or something nipped off between the crossed tips of bone.

Little rascal, he said.

Her mouth was filling up, she turned to the metal basin before he started singing again. *She's leaving now cos I just heard the slamming of the door* then humming. He didn't really know the words. She spat dark red and thick into the basin. When she resurfaced, he was looking at her and wiping his hands on something like a dishtowel.

Expect it'll bleed for a while, bound to be messy after that bother. Just take your time getting up. Take your time there. No rush.

She had slid to the edge of the chair, dunting the hooks and probes with having to hold on. The metal noise made her teeth sore. Her stomach felt terrible and she had to sit still, waiting to see straight.

Fine in a minute, he said. Wee walk in the fresh air. Wee walk back to school.

He finished wiping his hands and grinned, holding something out. A hard thing inside tissue. The tooth.

You made it, you have it haha. There you go. How's the jaw?

She nodded, and pointed to her mouth. This almost audible sound of a tank filling, a rising tide over the edges of the tongue.

Bleed for a while like I say. Don't worry though. Redheads always bleed worse than other folk. Haha. Sandra'll get you something: stop you making a mess of yourself.

Sandra was already away. He turned to rearrange the instruments she had knocked out of their neat arrangement on the green cloth.

Redheads, see. *Don't take your love to town.*

Maybe it was a joke. She tried to smile back till the blood started silting again. He walked over to the window as Sandra came back with a white pad in her hand. The pad had gauze over the top, very thick with a blue stripe down one side. Loops. A sanitary towel. The dentist was still turned away, looking out of the window and wiping his specs and talking. It took a minute to realize he was talking to her. It should stop in about an hour or so he was saying. Maybe three at the outside. Sandra pushed the pad out for her to take. If not by six o'clock let him know and they could give her a shot of something OK? Looking out the whole time. She tried to listen, tucking the loops at the ends of the towel in where they wouldn't be obvious, blushing when she put it up to her mouth. It was impossible to tell if they were being serious or not. The dentist turned back, grinning at the spectacles he was holding between his hands.

Sandra given you a wee special there. Least said haha. Redheads eh? *Oh Roooobeee*, not looking, wiping the same lens over and over with a cloth.

The fresh air was good. Two deep lungfuls before she wrapped her scarf round the white pad at her mouth and walked. The best way from the surgery was past the flats with bay windows and gardens. Some had trees, crocuses, and bits of cane. Better than up by the building site, full of those shouting men. One of them always shouted things, whistled loud enough to make the whole street turn and look. Bad enough at the best of times. Today would have been awful. This way was longer but prettier and there was nothing to stop her taking her time. She had permission. No need to worry about getting there for some particular ring of some particular bell. Permission made all the difference. The smell of bacon rolls at the café fetched her nose: coffee and chocolate. They spoiled when they reached her mouth, heaped up with sanitary towel and the blood still coming. Her tongue wormed toward the soft place, the dip where the tooth had been, then back between tongue root and the backs of her teeth. Thick fluid. A man was crossing the road, a greyhound on a thin lead, a woman with a pram coming past the phone box. Besides, girls didn't spit in the street. School wasn't that far though, not if she walked fast. She clutched the tooth tight in her pocket and walked, head down. The pram was there before she expected it; sudden metal spokes too near her shoes before she looked up, eyes and nose over the white rim of gauze. The woman not even noticing but keeping on, plowing up the road while she waited at the curb with her eyes on the gutter, trying hard not to swallow. Six streets and a park to go. Six streets.

The school had no gate, just a gap in the wall with pillars on either side that led into the playground. The blacked-out window was the staff room; the others showed occasional heads, some white faces watching. The music block was nearest. Quarter to twelve. It would be possible to wait in the practice rooms till the dinner bell in fifteen minutes and not shift till the afternoon. She was in no mood, though, not even for that. Not even for the music. It wouldn't be possible to play well. But there was no point in going home either because everything would have to be explained in triplicate when the mother got in and she never believed you anyway. It was all impossible. The pad round her mouth was slimy already, the wet going cold farther at the far sides. She could go over and ask Mrs McNiven for another towel and just go anyway, have a lie down or something but that meant going over to the other block, all the way across the playground again and the faces looking out knowing where you were going because it was the only time senior girls went there. And this thing round her mouth. Her stomach felt terrible too. She suddenly wanted to be in the music rooms, soothing herself with music. Something peaceful. Going there made her feel better just because of where it was. Not like at home. You could just go and play to your heart's content. That would be nice now, right now this minute, going up there and playing something: the Mozart she'd been working on, something fresh and clean. Turning, letting the glass door close, she felt her throat thicken, closing over with film. And that fullness that said the blood was still coming. A sigh into the towel stung her eyes. The girls' toilets were on the next landing.

Yellow. The light, the sheen off the mirrors. It was always horrible coming here. She could usually manage to get through the days without having to, waiting till she got home and drinking nothing. Most of the girls did the same, even just to avoid the felt-tip drawings on the girls' door —mostly things like split melons only they weren't. All that pretending you couldn't see them on the way in and what went with them, GIRLS ARE A BUNCH OF CUNTS still visible under the diagonal scores of the cleaners' Vim. Impossible to argue against so you made out it wasn't there, swanning past the word CUNTS though it radiated like a black sun all the way from the other end of the corridor. Terrible. And inside, the yellow lights always on, nearly all the mirrors with cracks or warps. Her own face reflected yellow over the nearside row of sinks. She clamped her mouth tight and reached for the towel loops. Its peeling away made her mouth suddenly cold. In her hand, the pad had creased up the center, ridged where it had settled between her lips and smeared with crimson on the one side. Not as bad as she had thought, but the idea of putting it back wasn't good. She wrapped it in three paper towels instead and stuffed it to the bottom of the wire bin under the rest, bits of paper and God knows what, then leaned over the sinks, rubbing at the numbness in her jaw, rinsing out. Big, red drips when she tried to open her mouth. And something else. She watched the slow trail of red on the white enamel, concentrating. Something slithered in her stomach, a slow dullness that made it difficult to straighten up again. Then a twinge in her back, a recognizable contraction. That's what the sweating was, then, the churning in her gut. It wasn't just not feeling well with the swallowing and imagining things. Christ. It wasn't supposed to be due for a week yet. She'd have to use that horrible toilet paper and it would get sore and slip about all day. Better that than asking Mrs McNiven for two towels, though, anything was better than asking Mrs McNiven. The cold tap spat water along the length of one blazer arm. She was turning it the wrong way. For a frightening moment, she couldn't think how to turn it off then managed, breathing out, tilting forward. It would be good to get out of here, get to something fresh and clean, Mozart and the white room upstairs. She would patch something together and just pretend she wasn't bleeding so much, wash her hands and be fit for things. The white keys. She pressed her forehead against the cool concrete of the facing wall, swallowing. The taste of blood like copper in her mouth, lips pressed tight.

The smallest practice room was free. The best one: the rosewood piano and the soundproofing made it feel warm.

There was no one in either of the other two except the student who taught cello. She didn't know his name, just what he did. He never spoke. Just sat in there all the time waiting for pupils, playing or looking out of the window. Anything to avoid catching sight of people. Mr Gregg said he was afraid of the girls and who could blame him haha. She'd never understood the joke too well but it seemed to be right enough. He sometimes didn't even answer the door if you knocked or made out he couldn't see you when he went by you on the stairs. It was possible to count yourself alone, then, if he was the only one here. It was possible to relax. She sat on the piano stool, hunched over her stomach, rocking. C-major triad. This piano had a nice tone, brittle and light. The other two made a fatter, fuzzier noise altogether. This one was leaner, right for the Mozart anyway. Descending chromatic scale with the right hand. The left moved in the blazer pocket, ready to surface, tipping something soft. Crushed tissue, something hard in the middle. The tooth. She had almost forgotten about the tooth. Her back straightened to bring it out, unfold the bits of tissue to hold it up to the light. It had a ridge about a third of the way down, where the glaze of enamel stopped. Below it, the roots were huge, matte like suede. The twist was huge, still bloody where they crossed. Whatever it was they had pulled out with them, the piece of skin, had disappeared. Hard to accept her body had grown this thing. Ivory. She smiled and laid it aside on the wood slat at the top of the keyboard, like a misplaced piece of inlay. It didn't match. The keys were whiter.

Just past the hour already. In four minutes the bell would go and the noise would start: people coming in to stake claims on the rooms, staring in through the glass panels on the door. Arpeggios bounced from next door. The student would be warming up for somebody's lesson, waiting. She turned back to the keys, sighing. Her mouth was filling up again, her head thumping. Fingers looking yellow when she stretched them out, reaching for chords. Her stomach contracted. But if she could just concentrate, forget her body and let the notes come, it wouldn't matter. You could get past things that way, pretend they weren't there. She leaned toward the keyboard, trying to be something else: a piece of music. Mozart, the recent practice. Feeling for the clear, clean lines. Listening. She ignored the pain in her stomach, the scratch of paper towels at her thighs, and watched the keys, the pressure of her fingers that buried or released them. And watching, listening to Mozart, she let the music get louder, and the door opened, the abrupt tearing sound of the doorseals seizing her stomach like a fist. The student was suddenly there and smiling to cover the knot on his forehead where the fear showed, smiling fit to bust, saying, Don't stop, it's lovely; Haydn isn't it? and she opened her mouth not able to stop, opened her mouth to say Mozart. It's Mozart—before she remembered.

Welling up behind the lower teeth, across her lips as she tilted forward to keep it off her clothes. Spilling over the white keys and dripping onto the clean tile floor. She saw his face change, the glance flick to the claw roots in the tissue before he shut the door hard, not knowing what else to do. And the bell rang, the steady howl of it as the outer doors gave, footfalls in the corridor gathering like an avalanche. They would be here before she could do anything, sitting dumb on the piano stool, not able to move, not able to breathe, and this blood streaking over the keys, silting the action. The howl of the bell. This unstoppable redness seeping through the fingers at her open mouth.

Scenes from the Life No. 23: Paternal Advice

It is a small room but quite cheery. There is an old-style armchair off to the left with floral stretch-covers and a shiny flap of mismatching material for a cushion. Behind that, a dark fold-down table, folded down. On the left, a low table surmounted by a glass bowl cut in jaggy shapes, containing keys, fuses, one green apple, and some buttons. Between these two is an orange rug and the fireplace. The fireplace is the focal point of the room. It has a wide surround of sand-colored tiles and a prominent mantelpiece on which are displayed a china figurine, a small stag's head in brass, a football trophy and a very ornate, heavy wrought-iron clock. On the lower part of the surround are a poker and a tongs with thistle tops and a matchbox. Right at the edge, a folded copy of the *Sunday Post* with the Broons visible on top. Behind the fireguard, the coals smoke with dross. The whole has the effect of calm and thoughtfulness. It is getting dark.

Place within this, the man SAMMY. He is perched on the edge of the armchair with his knees spread apart and his weight forward, one elbow on each knee for balance. He sits for some time, fists pressing at his mouth as he rocks gently back and forth, back and forth. We can only just hear the sound of a radio from next door, and the odd muffled thump on the wall. More noticeable than either of these is the heavy tick of the clock.

SAMMY exhales noisily. He appears to be mulling over some tricky problem. He is. But we are growing restless in the silence. Suddenly, too close, a noise like a radio tuning and we are in the thick of it.

> put it off long enough and it wasn't doing the boy any favors   just kidology to make out it was   just putting it off for himself more like   no   time to face it and get on with it   right   it was for the best after all and a father had to do his best by his boy even if it was hard even if he didn't want to   bad father that shirked his responsibilities no bloody use to anybody   the boy had to be learned right and learned right right from the word go   right   spare the rod   cruel to be nobody's fool that sort of thing right   christ tell us something we don't know

The man stands up abruptly, scowling.

> no argument it needed doing   just playing myself here it's HOW that's the thing that's the whole bloody thing is HOW   needed to be sure about these things tricky things needed to be clear in your mind before you opened your mouth else just make an arse of the whole jingbang just fuck it up totally TOTALLY aye got to be careful only one go at it right had to get it across in a oner and he had to learn it get the message right first time right had to know what you were at every word every move or else

SAMMY walks briskly to the window in obvious emotional agitation, bringing a dout from his right trouser pocket, then a box of matches. He inserts the dout off-center between his lips, takes a match from the box, feels for the rough side and sparks the match blind. The cigarette stump lights in three very quick, short puffs and still his eyes are focused on something we cannot see, outside the window in the middle distance. Up on tiptoes next, peering. Violent puffing. He shouts. BASTARDS! SPIKY-HEIDED BAS-TARDS. AD GIE THEM PUNK. WHAT DO THEY THINK THEY LOOK LIKE EH? JUST WHAT DO THEY THINK THEY'RE AT EH? and he is stubbing the cigarette butt out on the sill, turning sharply, going back to the easy chair to resume his perch. He runs one hand grease-quick through his hair from forehead to the nape of his neck and taps his foot nervously.

christ's sake get a grip eh remember what you're sup-posed to be doing eh   one think at a time   TIME the time must be getting on. Get on with it. Hardly see the time now dark already. Right. That's it then. That does it. Wee Sammy will be wondering what the hell is going on what his daddy is doing all this time.

SAMMY's eyes mist with sudden tears as the object of his sentimental contemplation appears in an oval clearing above the man's head. A thinks balloon. Inside, a small boy of about five or six years. He has ash-brown hair, needing cut, a thick fringe hanging into watery eyes that are rimmed pink as though from lack of sleep. It is WEE SAMMY. The balloon expands. WEE SAMMY in a smutty school shirt, open one button at the neck for better fit, and showing a tidemark ingrained on the inside. One cuff is frayed. The trousers are too big and are held up by a plastic snakebelt; badly hemmed over his sandshoes and saggy at the arse. He is slumped against the wall of what we presume to be the lobby. It is understandable his father is upset to think of him: he looks hellish. God knows how long the boy has been waiting there. The eyes, indeed the whole cast of the body suggest it may have been days. And still he waits as we watch.

SAMMY clenches his eyes and the balloon vision pops. *Pop.* Little lines radiate into the air to demonstrate with the word GONE in the middle, hazily. Then it melts too. The man makes a fist in his pocket but he speaks evenly. RIGHT. MAKE YOUR BLOODY MIND UP TIME. RIGHT. Then springs to the door where he steadies himself, smooths his hair back with the palm of his hand and turns the door-knob gently. A barless *A* of light noses in from the lobby with an elongated shadow of the boy inside. The man's face is taut, struggling to remember a smile shape. One hand still rests on the doorknob, the other that brushed back his hair reached forward, an upturned cup, to the child outside. A gesture of encouragement.

SAMMY: Come away in son.

The shadow shortens and the child enters, refocusing in the dim interior. The door clicks as his father closes it behind and the boy looks quickly over his shoulder. The man smiles more naturally now as if relaxing, and settles one hand awkwardly on the boy as they walk to the fireplace. Here, the man bobs down on his hunkers so his eyes are more at a level with his son's. WEE SAMMY's eyes are bland. He suspects nothing. The man has seen this too, and throughout the exchange to come is careful: his manner is craftedly diffident, suffused with stifled anguish and an edge of genuine affection.

SAMMY: (*Pause.*) Well. You're getting to be the big man
          now eh? Did your mammy say anything to you

about me wanting to see you? About what it was about?

WEE SAMMY: *Silence.*

SAMMY: Naw. Did she no, son? Eh. Well. It's to do with you getting so big now, starting at the school and that. You like the school?

WEE SAMMY: *Silence.*

SAMMY: Daft question eh? I didn't like it much either son. Bit of a waster, your da. Sorry now, all right. They said to me at the time I would be, telled me for my own good and I didn't listen. You'll see they said. Thought they were talkin rubbish. What did I know eh? Nothin. Sum total, nothin. Too late though! Ach, we're all the same. Anyway, what's this your da's tryin to say, you'll be thinkin. Eh. What's he sayin to me. Am I right?

WEE SAMMY: *Silence.*

SAMMY: Why doesn't he get on with it, is that what you're thinkin eh? Well this is me gettin on with it as fast as I can son. It's somethin I have to explain to you. Because I'm your daddy and because you're at the school and everythin. Makin your own way with new people. Fightin your own battles. I'm tryin to make sure I do it right son. It's like I was sayin about the school as well, about tellin you somethin for your own good. But I'm hopin you'll no be like me, that you'll listen right. And that's why I'm tellin you now. Now you're the big man but no too big to tell your daddy he's daft. Eh wee man?

SAMMY *rumples his son's hair proudly.* WEE SAMMY *smiles. This response has an instantly calming effect on the man and he raises himself up to his full height again. His voice needs to expand now to reach down to the boy. His demeanor is altogether more assured and confident.*

SAMMY: OK. That's the boy. Ready? One two three go.

WEE SAMMY *remains silent but nods up smiling at his father as* SAMMY *pushes his hands under the boy's oxters and lifts him up to near eye level with himself.*

SAMMY: Up you come. Hooa! Nearly too heavy for me now. You're the big fella right enough! Now. Here's a seat for you. No be a minute, then up on your feet.

He places his son on the mantelpiece between the brass ornament and the clock. He shifts the clock away to the low table, pats some stouriness off the shelf with the flat of his hand, then lifts the boy high, arms at full stretch, to reposition him in the center of the mantelpiece in place of the clock. The boy is fully upright on the mantelpiece.

SAMMY: Upsadaisy! Up we go!

WEE SAMMY: Dad!

SAMMY: What? What is it son? Not to take my hands away? Och silly! You're fine. On you come, stand up right, straighten your legs. Would I let you fall? Eh? That's my wee man, that's it. See? Higher than me now, nearly up to the ceiling. OK? Now, are you listening to me? Listen hard. I want you to do somethin for me. Will you do somethin for

me? Will ye son? Show me you're no feart to jump
eh? Jump. Jump down and I'll catch you.

*There is a long pause. The man is staring intently into the child's
eyes and the child's eyes search back. He is still tall on the mantelpiece among the china and brass ornaments, back and hand flat
against the wallpaper flora. The man's eyes shine.*

SAMMY: Show your daddy you're no feart son. I'll catch
you. Don't be feart, this is your da talkin to you.
Come on. For me. Jump and I'll catch you. Don't
be scared. Sammy, son, I'm waiting. I'm ready.

A few more seconds of tense silence click out of the clock. WEE
SAMMY *blinks. His hands lift from the wall and he decides: one
breath and he throws himself from the screaming height of the sill.
In the same second,* SAMMY *skirts to the side. The boy crashes
lumpily into the tiles of the fire surround. His father sighs and
averts his eyes, choking back a sob.*

SAMMY: Let that be a lesson to you son. Trust nae cunt.

Love in a
Changing
Environment

The bakery was how we found it. They gave us the address
and the bakery was right underneath the window, under
where we were moving in. Neither of us had much to bring.
We ferried clothes and a radio, two big cushions, cooking
things, and our bed linen along a tunnel of lukewarm pie,
gingerbread hearts, the sweet fat reek of doughnuts. The
bed last, mattress jamming up in the close-mouth, shutting
him in the dark and me on the other side, trapped in the
light and the crusty smell of split rolls. Lunchtime. Tuna
wholemeal and his laughter on the other side of the foam,
the mattress wresting from his unseen grip.

We had only one room and no clock. Hours shifted on white
toasters and morning rye to midmorning eccles cakes and
iced chelsea rounds. Crumpets and fruit scones, the crackling echo of cellophane, the sulphur stink of egg mayonnaise
led us through lunchtime and an hour with coffee at three
was signaled by the moist, animal vapor of cream me-
ringues. Our teatime table wafted with coffee kisses or cold
potato scones, the odd coconut castle: not our favorite time
of day. But with rising early, we seldom waited up long
after they closed. A few hours with warm milk by the

window, his watering the solitary fern, the fur-leaved African violet. Perhaps, he whispered, there would be flowers. We slept well, waiting for the early-morning drift of wholemeal.

Making love happened most often in the mornings, our bodies joining in a warm cloud of new-baked viennas and granary cobs from the shop beneath, the window hazy with hot chocolate croissants and our twin breaths. The scent of bread rising increased his thrust. Often he would tilt over my shoulder moaning as the oven doors opened in the kitchens beneath, his ejaculation impossible to hold back from the lure of working yeast. His semen usually parted company with me by the time they were shaping danish pastries. The surrounding air was everything and sweet.

The afternoon there was hammering nonstop from eleven till three, we had a mild disagreement. I said something unkind and went downstairs for two cheese rolls and an apple pie for later—we seldom cooked. It wasn't till the door refused I saw the sign. The bakery were selling up. We had toastless beans and cheddar at teatime and I blamed myself. Now I look back, there had been something different the whole morning. I looked up but he said nothing. He didn't think it his place to talk about relationships. An iced finger ran the length of my spine but I pushed it away. Without the companionship of the ovens downstairs, we felt disoriented and went to bed earlier than usual. He put out the light.

Next morning he took ages to come then went for a shower. I made porridge. He had a long walk before arriving home with milk. I found a baked-potato place and started bringing back tea in polystyrene cartons, the food chilling over. He quibbled with my choice of fillings and took things out on

the African violet's stubborn refusal to bloom, denying it
water. I tended it alone.

The new owners arrived almost a month later. We lay in
bed, wondering what the noise was, that dull slapping, the
flaccid thud of something thick splaying out against wood.
Then their smell, leaking into the room like gas. A butcher's
van sat below the window. The steady stench of gristle and
turning fat, dead tissue congested with blood became suddenly obvious. Our arms touched as we both turned away,
not sure what to say. I think we were afraid.

Over the week, sudden thuds and hacks began to punctuate
the hours, digging into soft wood. Time ticked on the cold
blue rend of joint and socket, the cracking of bone, the drill
and the saw. Silences afterward were worse, imagination
tensing for the soft sound of the scalpel, the suck of raw
muscle flenching from the blade, the lick of layer against
moist layer. Relaxation was difficult, sex worse. Mild pu-
trefaction hung like cigarette smoke under our ceiling and
clogged the close, attracting strays who bayed through the
still night, snuffling through the stained sawdust beneath
our window. Sometimes he went out without saying where
he was going, coming home with crumbs on his lapel. We
lost sleep and seldom touched, suspicious of the scent of
each other's skin. Each morning when the meat van arrived,
we fought over the shower, each eager for the sweet soap,
the gush of cleansing water. The day they unloaded the
bone grinder, I packed my bags.

Four streets distant, I moved into a new flat on the ground
floor smelling only of damp. Thinner and wiser, I eat no
meat and avoid cakes. The very sight of them makes me
sick.

Frostbite

Christ it was cold.

And only one glove as usual. The bare hand in the pocket, sweaty against the change counted out for the fare; the other inside the remaining glove, cramped stiff round the handle of the fiddle case. Freezing. Her feet were solid too; just a oneness of dead cold inside her boots in place of anything five-toed or familiar. She stamped them hard for spite, waiting and watching for the fingers of light smudging through the dark, the bus feeling its way up the other side of the hill. The last two had been full and driven straight on. No point getting angry. That was just the way of it.

Nothing yet.

Cloud came out of her mouth and she looked up. There on the other side of the road was the spire. Frame of royal blue, frazzled through with sodium orange, and the spire in the middle, lit from beneath by a dozen calendar windows: people working late. There was a hollow triangle of light above the tip; a clear opening in the sky where she could see the snow flurry and settle on the stone like white ivy. The university.

This was the best of the place now—the look of it. Still able to catch her out. As for the rest, it had not been what she had hoped. Her own fault, of course, expecting too much as usual. They said as much beforehand, over and over: it's no a job though, music willny keep you, it's no for the likes of you—cursing the teacher who had put the daft idea into her head in the first place. Still, she went, and she found they were right and they were not right. It wasn't her *likes* that bothered them, not that at all. Something much simpler. It was her excitement; all that gauche intensity about the thing. Total strangers wondered loudly who she was trying to impress. There was more than the music to learn: a whole series of bitter little lessons she never expected. It was hard. She learned to keep her ideas in check and her mouth shut, to carry her stifled love without whining much. But on nights like this, after compulsory practice that was all promise and no joy, cold and tired and waiting for a hypothetical bus, it was heavy and hard to bear. Even with her face to the sentimental spire, she wondered who it was she was trying to fool.

Low-geared growling turned her to the hill again. This time the effort paid off. Not one but two—jesus wasn't it always the way—sets of headlamps were dipping over the brow, coming on through the fuzzy evening smirr. She bounced the coins in her ungloved hand and watched as they nosed cautiously down through the slush. Then there was something else. A shape. A man lumping up and over the top of the hill, flapping after the buses. One was away already, had overtaken and gone ahead to let the other make the pickup. She stood while it braked and sat shivering at the stop, one foot on the platform to keep the driver and let the wee man catch up. The windows were yellow behind the steam. She looked to see if he was nearer and he stumbled, slittered to the gutter, fell. The driver revved the engine. The man lay on, not moving in the gutter like an old newspaper. The driver drew her a look. She shrugged, embarrassed. The bus began sliding out from under her foot. Too late already. There was nothing else for it. She settled the case in a drift at the side of the pole and turned and made a start, picking carefully up the hill toward the ragged shape still lying near the gutter. An arm flicked out. She came nearer as he struggled onto his hands and knees, trying to stand. Then he crashed down again on the thin projections of his backside and groaned, knees angled up, fingers clutching at his brow in a pantomime of despair. By the time she reached him he was bawling like a wean. She could see blood congealed, red jam squeezing between the fingers. The line of his jaw was grey.

OK?
The man said nothing. Just kept sobbing away. He was a fair age too.
OK eh? What happened to you grandad?

She had never called anybody grandad in her life. And that voice. Like a primary teacher or something. She started to blush. Maybe she should get him onto his feet instead. Touch would calm him down and he might stop greeting to concentrate. She looked about first to check if there was another witness, hoping for a man. A man who would be shamed by her struggling on her own and come and do the thing for her, leave her clucking on the sidelines while he took over. But there was no one and she knew she had called the thing upon herself anyway. Fools rushed in right enough.

An acrid smell of drink, wool and clogged skin rose as she bent toward him, and she saw the knuckles scraped raw, the silted nails. Closing her eyes, she linked his arm and started pulling, hoping for the best. They must look ridiculous.

C'mon then, let's get you up. Need to get up. Catch your death sitting in the wet like this. Come on, up.

He acquiesced, childlike, letting himself be hauled inelegantly straight before he finished the rest for himself. He backed onto a low wall and waited while he caught his breath. O thanks hen, between wheezes, words vaporizing in the cold. Am that ashamed, all no be a minute but am that ashamed. All be fine in a minute. Am OK hen.

He didn't look OK. He looked lilac and the sodium glare didn't do him any favors. He puffed on about being fine and ashamed while she foraged in her pocket for a paper hanky to pat at the bloody jelly on his temple, the sticky threads stringing across to his nose. She thought better of it and gave it to him instead—something to do, shut him up for a minute, maybe. But neither the idea nor the mopping up worked too well. His hand stopped at his brow only as long as she held it there. When he saw what it produced the whine started again. O my god hen, o hen . . . see . . . o look at that, as he dabbed and looked, dabbed and looked.

You're fine, fine. Just a wee bit surprised, that's all. Take your time and just relax OK? Relax. Where is it you're going anyway?
He kept patting and looked at her. Very pale eyes, coated like a crocodile's, the sockets overbig.

O he'll be that angry hen. He will and am that ashamed. Am a stupit old fool a am. Nothing but a stupit old man. The pale eyes threatened to leak. Who? Who'll be angry?

The trick was to keep him talking and standing up. Every time he stumbled, he repeated what he'd just said. Between repetitions, she found he had been due at his son's house, due at a particular time and he was late. They were supposed to be going somewhere. It sounded like a pub. They were to set off from the son's house and he was chasing the bus because he was already late did she see? She tried to.

Och he'll not be mad. Just tell him you were running for the bus and you fell. How will that get him angry? You'll be fine.

He wasn't content yet. The specs but. A broke the specs hen.

There was a lull. She looked about the tarmac and the pavement. There weren't any specs. Then his hand was into his pocket, fumbling out three pieces of plastic and glass: See? She broke ma specs.

She. He said *she; she* broke the specs. Right enough, that couldn't have happened just now. There had to be more to it, and she knew already she didn't want to hear it. All she had wanted was to make sure he was all right, get him on his feet and back on his way. But this was what she was getting and it was difficult to get out of now. It was her that had started it, her choice to come up that hill. This was part of it now.

Who broke your specs?

She knew it had to happen and it did. He started to cry. He howled for a good minute or so while she cursed silently and patted clumsily at his sleeve, shooshing. He caught enough breath to hiccup out some more: It's ma own fault hen. It was a bad woman, a bad woman. She hit me hen, o she killed me. She had to smile. The exaggeration wasn't just daft, it was reassuring too. He couldn't see her anyway.

Still, even as she told him he was fine, fine, she knew there was more coming she wasn't going to like. The story. A man's story about what he would call a *bad woman*, and he would tell it as though she wasn't a woman herself, as if she shared his terms. As though his were the only terms. And she wouldn't be expected to argue—just stand and listen. The smiling didn't last long. He told her about a pub, having a drink, then a bad woman, something about a bad woman but he hadn't known it at the time, and as they were leaving the pub together, going out the door, she hit him. Knocked him down in the street, hard, so it broke his specs. When he reached that part he gazed down at the bits he held in his hand, taking in the fact with a deep sigh that exhaled as cursing and swearing. He whooered and bitched till he was unsteady on his legs again then started whining. He was a stupit old fool and a silly old man, should never have had anything to do with the bad woman. Bad bad bitchahell. Then there were more tears.

She hadn't reacted once. And maybe it was worth it. He seemed steadier, ready to make off again for the stop. She let him walk, moving slowly alongside to keep him straight while he muttered and sobbed about himself. She knew better than to ask but she wondered, step by step, steering him downhill. She wanted to know about the woman. What had he said to make her do that? Was that when he had been cut—where the blood had come from? It must have happened right enough: he would hardly make a thing like that up. But it was hard to imagine this sorry, sniveling wee man provoking it, being pushy or lewd-mouthed. It was in another place though, with another woman altogether. He could have been different. And he must have done something. Unless of course there really were such bad women that went about hitting old men for nothing. What the hell was a *bad woman* anyhow—was it a prostitute he meant? The corner of her eye caught his face, the mottled purple skin under grey veins and a big dreep at the end of his nose. The very idea turned her stomach. Yet she couldn't stop her chest being sore for the stranger: he seemed so beaten, so genuinely surprised by what had hit him not just once but twice that day. He was still muttering when they reached the stop: broke ma specs, cow. She felt her jaw sore with remembering to be quiet. Shhh.

Shh, forget about her eh? She's away now, forget about it. Let's just get you to your boy's place. Get you on the bus.
What else could she do?
Canny be up to them hen. She realized this was a confidence. Advice. Canny be up to them. A bad lot.
Aye, a lot of it about. What bus is it you get?
Aye, don't you worry. Get the bus. All be fine in a minute, get the bus.

There was no point in keeping asking, best just to wait with him. The right bus would come and he would recognize it instinctively. Fair enough. Holding some of the weight, she kept her arm under his: the wet frosting on his sleeve burned the fingers of her gloveless hand. He was looking down at something, staring as though to work out what it was.

Violin hen. Eh—violin? Nice, a violin. A like that stuff, classical music and that.
She shook her head thinking about it. Victorian melodrama as they chittered in the twilight under the university spire —Hearts and Flowers. But she said nothing. Knew enough by this time not to respond to remarks, even harmless ones, about being *on the fiddle* or *doing requests*, or any of the other fatuous to obscene things some men assumed a lassie car-

rying a violin case was asking for. Anyway, the bus was coming now: she could hear it. Good timing. She turned for the pleasure of watching it approach: twin haloes of deliverance.

This one do you? A fifty-nine?
She couldn't hear his answer for the searing of brakes. He seemed ready enough to get on, though; his hands stretching out full, paddling toward the pole to prepare for the assault on the platform. She shunted the case to one side with her foot and moved with him. The conductress hauled while she pushed till he was inside, clutching the pole. Then he swiveled suddenly to face her.

Cheerio hen and a have ti thank you very much, very much indeed. Yiv been kind ti me yi have that. He was leaning out dangerously and shaking her hand uncomfortably tightly in both of his, the pole propping his chest. She nodded in what she hoped was a reassuring way, weary. She hadn't the heart left to explain she had meant to get on too, this was her bus as well. She just kept patting and shaking at his hand; giving up to it. She felt daft enough already and it would take forever to pantomime through. She wasn't in any hurry, could easily wait for the next one. Parting shot then. What's the name? What do they call you eh?
The conductress and driver looked but the engine continued to purr neutrally. Her smile was as much for them: indulge it a wee bit longer?

Me? He was pleased. Pat, am Pat Gallagher hen. Pat.

Cheerio then Pat. See and look after yourself a wee bit better in future eh?
His face changed then, remembering. He hesitated for a second, baring his teeth, then he spat, suddenly vicious.

Aye. Keep away from bastart women, thats what yi do. Filth. Dirty whooers and filth the lot of them, the whole bloody lot. Get away fi me bitchahell—and he lunged a fist. It wasn't well-aimed and she had enough of a glimpse to see it come. It didn't connect: just made her totter back a few steps; enough for the driver to seize this as his moment and drive off, chasing an already sliding schedule.

She stood on the pavement and watched till it went round the corner, then stood on watching the space where it had been. After a moment, she shut her mouth again and pulled up her coat collar. Warm enough now: just as well there was no one about, though she looked round to check and shrugged to be casual just in case. The spire was still there across the road; still beautiful, still peaceful. Snow feathered about and nothing moved behind the gates. No difference. Thankful, she leaned back against the stop: it would be a while yet. Then she remembered the case and stooped to lift it out of the snow, leaving a free-standing drift where it had been. Didn't want it to get too cold, go out of tune. Not as though it was her own. Then, unexpectedly, she felt angry; violently, bitterly angry. The money in her pocket cut into her hand. Who did he think he was, lashing out at people like that? And what sort of bloody fool was she, letting him? What right had he? What right had any of them? She'd show him. She'd show the whole bloody lot of them. Shaking, she snatched up the fiddle case and glared at the hill. To hell with this waiting. There were other ways, other things to do. Take the underground; walk, dammit. Walk.

She crossed the road, defying the slush underfoot, making a start up the other side of the hill.

Scenes from the Life No. 29: Dianne

From a first-floor window, a woman with a baby looks down over the street being dug up, full of pits and craters. Two different men, just outside the bus stop, just able to be seen, are talking. You wait in the shelter of the bus stop watching them let buses past, noticing they talk too loud, giggling low in the throat in unpredictable places, making wide sudden gestures with their hands.

so he's two days aff the rigs right, two days aff wi this two hundred quid fuckin two hundred NOTES christ NOTES fuckin FISTload right he says are yous comin he says so we goes aye and he gets these TAXIS right these TAXIS ti the pub christ pub ti pub right wan efter the fuckin next yin and there's EVERYTHIN right this lagers an brandies an christnoze ken how he canny HANDLE the drink right canny HANDLE it well he's drinking these brandies an lagers an fuckin chamPAGNE chamPAGNE christ teQUILA for fucksake teQUILA techrist and he COULD haud it man that's the funny thing right and he COULD fuckin haud it, the money, the life then it's

Neither of the men is older than twenty-five. One of them could easily be eighteen. Their hair is gelled and styled, the cuts neat, shaped at the napes of their white necks, their chins rough with bristle. Stroking would leave scores. You try not to think about that, watching the road. The road is full of pits and craters.

dancin boys DANcin so we jist looks right then he's ach moan up the DANcin an fuckin away so we FOL-LOWS him right we FOLLOWS him aff the bus up the STAIRS man these STAIRS fuckin STAIRS to the hoose fourth fuckin flair christ and in the lobby right and he STARTS right he STARTS wi this WEAN fuckin wean in the livin room sittin this lassie christ pickin her up fuckin PICKIN her up and she's greetin right squealin he's throwin her up then the bastard's away jist WOOF right WOOF wan minute he's there then AWAY FOR A SHOWER BOYS fuck an we're left wi the wee fuckin lassie left wi the wean christ the NEXT THING he's

The shelter smells of melting plastic, dogs in the rain. Trying not to look aware, not to look conscious. Across the road, different men drill a deep trench, filling the whole street with noise, a heavy underground bore that comes and finds you even here, buzzing through the soles of your shoes. One smiles across at the talkers who see nothing but each other. There is no bus in the distance.

comes back wi this T-SHIRT this short fuckin wet fae the shower this T-SHIRT, the wyes it's the WEIGHT TRAININ boys he says LOOK so we looks while he's flexin the muscles this T-fuckin-shirt oot the FEEL IT he says and the wee lassie feart wi the noise he says FEEL IT ti christ so we're touchin the muscles jist

touchin he turns an he's oot wi this stick christ big
fuckin cue right WOOF roon his heid like a WOOF
fuckin caber or somethin nearly RIGHT IN THE EYE
I says WOOF fuckin COOL IT jist WOOF lassie
screamin he's taken his T-shirt this TAP fuckin tap aff
this sweat like an hoor an this TAP aff an christ he says
LOOK fuckin shouts and this build some build
tatTOO oan his chest fucking HEART through the
core an DI-
ANNE it says jeez fuck DI-
ANNE

And the woman with the baby goes on looking down. But
only at you. Only at you.

it was

It was toward evening and the color was seeping from the grass verge under her feet. Two-story council terraces with frames of paint borders round the windows, flaking like late-in-the-day eyeliner, lined the opposite side of the road; behind her, a straggling T-junction split the erratic paths of children and women following the ground home with headscarves and late shopping. Both sides of the road had verges with lampposts, furred in their own bleachy light, and small close-stacked houses. None of the buildings was new.

Older couples would be sitting on the scratchy roses of their ancient settees inside watching slot telly—its blue-flickering familiarity was throbbing against dark sideboards: flame buds would be growing on coals still smoking with newness in the grates. She could hear Eamonn Andrews telling them that *This Was Their Life*. Seven o'clock?

She wasn't sure if she knew this place or not. Something was homely about it, something that though not kent was not strange. With effort, she turned her gaze down to her feet and the sepia grass; her verge neighbored the dull macadam of the road to the edge of her vision at what must be the crest of a hill. Then, it would roll down out of sight and tumble on till it reached the sea. Overwhelmed, she knelt to feel the cling of the cool blades wrap the bare skin of her knees, exposed between long socks and dark grey skirt. Her eyes closed, near to weeping with the pleasure of it. Suddenly she was afraid, in panic at the foolishness of her joy and that someone might witness it. Surely she was too old for this kind of thing (her eyes felt wrinkled with strain) she opened them quickly

and found herself standing at the now-grey privet hedge of one of the smarter pebble-dashes on the corner, her hands resting on the stubby hardness of cropped branches. It smelled of twilight and being outside. Scented stock wafted up sickly from underneath it. Gradually aware of their dull ache, she lifted her palms, pitted from the striving of the blunt-edged bush, and slid them into jacket pockets. Inside, her nails trapped crumbs, vying with them for the corners, for it was now blue-dark and getting noticeably chillier.

then the glitter of it caught her eye

then the glitter of it caught her eye

There was
something shiny in the earth at the foot of the wall, just under the drainpipe and less than half-hidden. It was at the foot of the facing roughcast, across the patch of stock. The hedge pushed at her blazer. Her hand was on the drainpipe, a clod of thick rust tapped her shoe: to stoop to look she knelt

she knelt to pick it up

it was

Dusty, trailing crumbs from her pockets, her fingers—now quite dull with warmth—found its edges and curled under. The smell of the earth lifted as it parted to free one corner.

She knelt to pick it up
It was a face. A little crusted and with eyes shut tight against encroaching dirt: a little flattened from having lain there its indeterminate time and being pressed against the concrete slabs. Her body and her breathing were smooth and calm though her eyes ticked seconds round the rim of it.

Pushing her lips apart and outward, she puffed feeble breath at the closed lids. Then more boldly she began to pick at the half-hard veil of mud with the unclean nail of her right index finger, clasping the whole face in her left hand with its cheek nestled in the flesh cup of her palm. As the flakes fell away, the skin showed pink and surprisingly clean beneath and she became more intent on the task. Most concentration and skill would be needed where the dirt crowded thickest in ridges at the creases of its eyes. She had to change tactic, retracting the nail and brushing with a plump pad of fingertip instead. This seemed better: the silt crumbled and parted fairly dryly to slide out of the cracks it had claimed. She blew gently again to help its progress. There was a sucking sound and an intake of air. Her eyes snapped wide and lips drew back their kiss. It was

The little man smiled as he took her elbow. There was no need to acknowledge anything unusual in the situation for nothing was.

Come on and we'll go for a cup of tea

Immediate bittersweet stab of recognition at a voice forgotten—how long? Her whole heart seemed to move with pity for the wee figure already making off toward a kettle. The still lamplight outlined his bald head and traced the grey nightcolor of his cheek where it moved to prepare another sentence of encouragement for her to come. It was a rough cheek, hairily whitened with stubble that had alternately fascinated and horrified her as a child; she felt its jaggy trail scratch a skirl of wild shrieking from an infant mouth, her eyes stretched golly-wide in excitement. *Too much excitement for the wean.*

Uncle George.
Uncle George.

he was
He was walking ahead.
It's freezing. Come on and we'll get a heat.

She wanted to do something kind and wonderful for this, the swell of her heart now intolerable, but she couldn't think what. Not quickly enough, anyway. What was clear, though, was that it was now her due to be as gentle as she could for him. He had no awareness that he was dead and she would not let him know. So he should not suspect or have to hesitate for her, she spurred to movement then—a rush to reaffirm his short, bulky presence. They went jauntily and quietly, lured by the steamy warmth of the promised tea and its milky sweetness. She knew he wouldn't live far away.

David

I hated the miss thing and anyway I never taught any of them, not in class; just jokes with Colin and Marie, the couple, Sam like a big farmer's boy and David, sullen behind the blond fringe needing cut. You never knew what he was thinking. There was an afternoon once he came to the classroom door, his face blotted out with the sun at his back only the blue eyes there like something unnatural, unnatural blue. He made me break sweat.

It was last day. They were meeting at Sam's house: cheaper than the pub and his parents were out for the night so he felt free. Funny thinking about parents and being accountable: it reminded you they were just kids really, just kids at the school, the boys hardly needing to shave. So we went there, me and Carol the only teachers into uncharted territory, Sam's parents being away. We handed over the two bottles of cider and he said Kid's drink, cider: too juvenile. They were drinking already out of these little glasses, no more than pub measures; whisky and sherry like after-dinner guests. Sam took the cider to the kitchen, these bottles of cider that were such a joke. David wasn't there so we sat together with Colin and Marie, the couple, making conversation in fits and starts. Then the doorbell rang and I knew I was waiting for it: the voice in the hall, clinking of bottles. I knew it was him because my hands were sweating. The back of my neck and upper lip. I went to the stereo and turned it up louder leaving Carol with the talking. I'm not good with small talk anyway. Then the boys came through. We were all drinking out these tiny glasses and getting over not being used to each other. It was better when I took off my jacket and sat on the floor with a can that tasted bad but made me relaxed. I changed the music every so often, consciously joining in. I hate parties. But it was a quiet kind of good time we were having, very domestic. Sam had even made sandwiches jesuschrist as if we were proper grown-ups I said, and passed them round. It got noisier, turning the music up when we drank some more. I hadn't eaten so I suppose it was going straight into the bloodstream because I was dizzy when I stood up. I sat next to Carol with Colin and Marie, the couple: Sam and David arguing about something pointless in the armchairs. Cosy. It was nice to be included, their just tipping seventeen. Also I might never see them again. That was what this was about. I must have been rubbing my collar at the breastbone like a nervous tic: crossing and uncrossing my legs. I must have been doing something because the next thing Sam was having to change the record. And David was looking at me. He was looking me right in the eye from the chair, leaning forward and braceleting the glass with one hand, the silver watchband clicking on the rim. Sam was telling a joke, Colin and Marie laughing. But he was looking with his eyes level. I could feel his watching even with my head turned away. My hand must have lost the grip on the can. Lager was seeping on my blouse, the lace edge of the bra starting to show through and the shock of cold getting warmer. I wondered afterward if I did it on purpose. But there was this spreading wetness and the cushion under my skirt burning.

I had to stand up and Sam said he would show me where I could sponge the mark at the sink upstairs. I'll find it, I said, I'll find it, shaky when I walked because I knew what was going to happen. I heard David saying I'll go. I heard him saying it: it's all right. I'll go.

The hall was cooler. I stopped to let him catch up, waiting partway up the stairs. He slid past so our hips touched as he went ahead. Oops he said like a little boy. Oops. Seven more steps and he stopped in front of me, waiting at the bathroom door. My stomach went tight as I turned but smiled saying it was all right for something to say while he put his hand out, pushing the door for me to go on inside. We stopped. Just stood not going forward or back, waiting, my stomach knotting like a fist. The lace moved under the stained blouse. The ripple of my own breast.

His palm was clammy. I touched once. Then he laced his fingers into mine till they were tight. The wood at the side of the door biting my spine. He came closer so slow I wasn't sure if he would or

Our teeth touched, mouths open. I felt him swallow, the skin on my lip stretch till it split, a sudden give from the tightness and I was sliding my hands, tugging on the thin shirt: ridges of warm rib beneath my fingers rubbing my palms on the warm sides of his jeans, the length of seam. He pulled his head back and looked, the blue eyes and smooth temples. Flecks of blond on the backs of his hands, his nails trailed over the blouse, the nipple stiffening where he let his hand wait and I said something I don't remember. I don't remember. Then there was my mouth on his neck, salt nipping the torn skin of my lip. And we weren't kissing anymore, just falling back, the pile of the carpet reaching then pushing through the thin stuff of my blouse and I was

arching like a bridge, searching for the zip through the stiff
denim, feeling the weight of him fall closer and the blouse
sliding to my neck as he pushed under the cloth for one
breast. His hardness, stiff, hard smoothness in my hand.
Our mouths separate now, a nudging between my legs with
one knee and his shift into place as my hand opened, the
warm tip wet on my thigh. The slip of a single vertebra.
And he entered sudden and hard not like a man but guileless,
his hair falling into my eyes till by the time I was sure what
we had done he shivered and cut like an engine, the other
heart thumping on my chest and not being able to think or
stop my eyes, not being able. And there was Sam's voice
calling from downstairs if we were all right, was I all right?
Calling his name, not being able to catch my breath while
I wondered, eyes splintering, wondering
what else to say
what else to say

Two Fragments

I remember two things in particular about my father. He had ginger hair and two half fingers on one hand. The ring finger and the middle one fastened off prematurely at the knuckle, like the stumpy tops of two pink pork links, but smoother. They were blown off during the war. This was a dull sort of thing, though; my mother had another story that suited my child-need far better.

It started with the usual, your daddy in the pub. I could've had a mint of money today if he hadn't been a drinker by the way. Anyway he'd been in there all night and he came out the pub for the last bus up the road, but by the time he staggered to the stop he was just in time to see it going away without him. He chased it but it wasn't for stopping. He'd missed it. There was nothing for it but to start walking. He had to go along past Piacentini's on the corner and that was where he smelt the chips. It wasn't all that late yet and they were still open. The smell of the chips was a great thing on a cold night and with all the road still to go up and he just stood there for a wee while soaking up the warm chips smell. It made him that hungry he thought he had to go in and get some, so he counted all the loose change in his pockets and with still having the bus fare he just had enough.

He was that drunk though he dropped all the money and he had to crawl about all over the road to get it all back because he needed every penny to get the chips. That took him a wee while. And by the time he finally got in, Mrs Piacentini was just changing the fat and so he had to wait. That was all right but the smell of the chips was making him hungry by this time. Just when he was about to get served, a big polisman came in and asked for his usual four bags and because he was in a hurry and he was a regular he got served the chips that were for your daddy. So by the time he was watching the salt and vinegar going onto his bag, his mouth was going like a watering can. He was starving. The minute he got out into the street with them, he tore open the bag and started eating them with his fingers, stuffing them into his mouth umpteen at a time and swallowing them too fast. He thought they were the best chips he had ever tasted. He was that carried away eating them that it wasn't till he went to crumple up the empty bag and fling it away he saw the blood. When he looked over his shoulder there was a trail of it all the way up the road from Piacentini's. He was that hungry he'd eaten two of his fingers for chips with salt and vinegar.

My granny had a glass eye. She was a fierce woman. A face like a white gingernut biscuit and long, long grey hair. She smoked a clay pipe. And she had this glass eye.

My grandfather was a miner, and the miners got to take the bad coal, the stuff with the impurities the coal board weren't allowed to sell. She built up the fire one day and was bashing a big lump of this impure coal with the poker when it exploded and took her eye out. So there was another story about that. Again, it was my mother's: I was much too feart for my granny to ask her anything.

Your granny could be awful cruel sometimes. She drowned cats. She drowned the kittens and if the cats got too much she drowned them as well. There was one big tom in particular used to come up the stairs and leave messes in the close. Gad. Right outside your door and everything. Stinking the place out. I don't like tomcats and neither did your granny. She got so fed up with the rotten smell and its messes that one day she decided she was going to get rid of it. So she laid out food and when it came to eat the food she was going to sneak up on it with a big bag. It was that suspicious, watching her the whole time while it was eating: your granny staring at the cat and the cat staring back. It was eating the food in the one corner and your granny was hovering with the bag in the other. High Noon. Anyway, she waited for her minute and she managed to get it. Not right away, though. It saw her and jumped, but it went the wrong way and got itself in a corner and she finally managed to get the bag over it. By the time she got into the kitchen, with the cat struggling in the bag, she was a mass of scratches. The cat was growling through the bag and trying to get its claws through at her again, so she held up the bag and shook it to show it who was the boss. Then she didn't know what to do next, till she clapped eyes on the boiler. A wee, old-fashioned boiler like a cylinder thing on wee legs with a lid at the top. She got a string and tied up the top of the bag and then she dropped the cat right into the boiler drum. It was empty, of course. She was going to keep it in there till the boys came back (that's your uncle Sammy and uncle Alec) and get one of them to take it to the tip and choke it or something. She was fed up with it after all that wrestling about. She got on with her work in the kitchen, and as she was working about she could hear the cat banging about in the boiler the whole time, trying to get out, while she was getting on with the dinner and boiling up kettles of water for the boys coming home for their wash. When they got in from their work, the first thing they did was get a wash: there was no baths in the pit and they never sat down to their tea dirty. Your granny wouldn't let them. So they came right into the kitchen when they got home and the first thing they noticed was this thumping coming out the boiler. Alec says to her what the hell's that mother and she tells them about the tomcat. Just at that the thing starts growling as if it's heard them and our Sammy says I hope you don't think I'm touching that bloody thing, listen to it. And he starts washing at the sink and laughing like it was nothing to do with him. Even our Alec wouldn't go and lift the lid. So she got quite annoyed and rolled her sleeves up to show them the scratches to tell them she wasn't feart for it and she would do it herself. So after she'd gave them their tea, she got them out the kitchen so she could get on with it.

She had thought what she was going to do. First, she got two big stones from the coalhouse and the big coal bucket from the top of the stair. She put the bricks at the boiler side and filled the big bucket with cold water at the sink. The cat had stopped making so much noise by this time so it was probably tired. This would be a good time. She got the washing tongs, the big wooden things for lifting out the hot sheets after they'd been boiled, and went over to the boiler, listening. Then she flung back the lid, reached in quick with the tongs and pulled the bag out before the cat knew what was happening. The minute it was out the drum, though, it starts thrashing about again and your granny drops the bag and runs over to the sink for the pail, heaves it over to the boiler and pours the whole lot in. She filled it right up nearly to the top. The bag was scuffling about the floor so she waited till it went still again. Then when it had stopped moving, she gets hold of it with the tongs quick and plonks it straight into the water, banging the lid down shut and the bricks on top.

She went straight into the living room to build up the fire and tell the boys she'd managed fine without them, quite pleased with herself. She would just leave the cat in the boiler till the next morning to be sure it was drowned and get the bucket men to take it away. Sammy was a bit offended. He said she was a terrible woman but they didn't do anything about the poor bloody cat so they were just as bad. There was no noise in the kitchen when they went for a wash before they went to their bed. It was a shame.

Well it was still the same thing the next morning when your granny went in to light the kettle. Nothing coming out the boiler. That was fine. She got me and Tommy away to the school and your uncle Alec and Sammy were away to the pit and our Lizzie was out as well. So that was her by herself and she started getting the place ready for the disposal of the body. She put big sheets of newspaper all round the floor and got the tongs ready. It would be heavy. She shifted one of the bricks off the boiler lid and listened to make sure. Nothing. She shifted the other one off and lifted up the lid. There was a hellish swoosh and the cat burst out the boiler, soaking to the bone, its eyes sticking right out its head. It must've fought its way out the bag and been swimming in there all night, paddling and keeping just its nose above the water, and the minute it saw the light when your granny lifted the lid, it just threw itself up. It shot out straight at her face and took her eye out just like that. Your granny in one corner of the kitchen, with the eye in another and the tomcat away like buggery down the stairs.

Fingers for the army.
An eye for the coal board.
A song and dance for the wean.

Scenes from the Life No. 26: The Community and the Senior Citizen

A sudden flash, some half-hearted flickering. A three-sided box. It is a compact living room and the chief impression is one of brightness. Yes, a lot of afternoon sunlight is forcing in from somewhere off to the left. It spreads on the pale wallpaper like transparent butter and creates a long rhombus of itself on the carpet; a contained shape from the toomuchness of outside. Much of the floral tracery of the carpet is lost inside it and the pink design is clear only at the fitted extremities. There are no shadows in the corners, only a neat standard lamp with a plain shade, a green wicker chair.

Two very white doors complete the harmony of the composition. They hang as balances on the center of the facing wall, radiating a high, professional gloss, the more noticeable for their being so close together. On the strip between, some five feet from the white skirting, a square frame reflects fiercely. The picture or photograph behind the glass is almost entirely glared out by bars of light on the surface; but something dark seems to be whispering up through the sheen as of a black-and-white still. We may assume a wedding photograph rather than linger.

On the right, another door, fractionally ajar, and a low table with an empty glass bowl: opposite, near the light source and pale grey curtains, an empty display cabinet. Details obtained by absorption, for our eyes have become used to the decibel level of light and are veering naturally to the main interest in the middle of the room.

Centered squarely toward us is a large, dove-grey settee. A fine stripe shaved into its plain velvet pile makes three sections of the whole and these, in turn, are bisected by the lightshape from the window, washing the left of the settee paler than the right. Just within the shaded part, a solid figure bulks down the cushions, spoiling the symmetry. Swathed in navy blue, it is the only dark thing in the room. The lower buttons of the coat are undone, revealing a wedge of blue skirt and plump orange legs stretching down to flat black shoes. There is a scant navy hat on her short auburn hair, a black shoulder bag resting at one hip. Ah. It is the HEALTH VISITOR. A young woman, her face is full and smooth, her lips ripe and dark from recent applications of warm porcelain; she has been drinking tea. The cup relaxes in one pink palm—the left. The other hand sports a fragment of gingernut biscuit (a pleasing color halfway between that of her hair and legs) which she waves as she talks. For though we cannot hear, she is talking: her head nods and her mouth moves. The angle of her gaze and that moving mouth prompt a glance in their direction. Yes, there is someone in the companion chair now we look. Feel free; she cannot know we are watching.

It is an OLD WOMAN. Three quarters in profile, her body conveys an uncomfortable blend of rigidity and exhaustion.

Feet and knees brace tightly together, swollen ankles jowling over the lip of her slippers, yet her torso slumps and her neck droops over quite hypothetical breasts. Certainly, she is thin; torturously thin: limbs emerge as skinbound sinew from the hems of her clothes. The clothes themselves, a knitted skirt and top in neutral tones, are dull and undistinguished—flesh color—though nothing like her own. Her skin is uniformly pale, a waxy cream-yellow without blemish. The hands that for the moment spread from cuff-ends to over the dove-grey armrests seem painted over, or squeezed into surgical gloves. They seem not to possess fingernails. Her hair is no more reassuring: a frazzle of neglected vanity with pale roots and raggedy red-grey ends sticking up untidily like half-rinsed paintbrushes. Beneath hangs her face, and, more obviously, her mouth. It gapes. And there are silver trails at its corner. Occasionally, she makes a tentative dab at the runnel of saliva, but the sheen seems to vanish only long enough for another thread to form and ooze back along the same path to her chin. The eyes, too, shift continually from side to side, suggesting a nervous or ingrained habit. She has certainly let herself go.

Between the two of them is a low table strewn with tea things—an empty cup and saucer, a second saucer and teaspoon, an opened carton of milk and a blue plate with one remaining gingernut. It seems they have been sitting for some time.

The HEALTH VISITOR stirs. The scent of the room rises—a faint cloy of earth and cold meat we had not noticed before. Now there is a soft scuffling as the HEALTH VISITOR uncrosses her plump legs, the creak of the settee, then the dry click of the cup against the saucer as she sets it down. Someone increases the volume further.

HEALTH VISITOR: No other visitors tonight then? Just yourself?

OLD WOMAN: *Silence. Shakes her head and dabs at her mouth.*

HEALTH VISITOR: But everything's fine just the same? Keeping well eh? I say you're keeping well.

OLD WOMAN: *Silence.*

HEALTH VISITOR: That's good. All the messages in for the weekend—nothing I can get you?

OLD WOMAN: *Silence. Nods her head and moves her lips.*

HEALTH VISITOR: It's good to see you're keeping yourself busy anyway. Keeping busy eh?

Throughout this exchange, the OLD WOMAN has been struggling with her face and now manages to make a slack oblong of her mouth with lips parted and some teeth showing in the divide. Once attained, its maintenance is no easy matter. The grimace is tight, cutting creases into her cheeks and her dribbling is markedly worse. But she holds it there, and through its effortful set dredges up her voice and an answer.

OLD WOMAN: Try to.

HEALTH VISITOR: Good for you. Good for you, Mrs Maule. Pity there aren't more like you. Well, we know don't we. It's up to yourself in the last analysis, isn't it?

The HEALTH VISITOR has begun to wrestle up from the settee, clutching her bag then standing to smooth down the creases and crumbs from the navy coat, restoring her authority. It is a signal. The OLD WOMAN takes it to begin her own procedure for rising, grasping the armrests with whitening knuckles, bracing her feet and pushing, pushing till finally she is erect. And all the while she has managed to support the grim rictus we now know for a smile; holds it and strengthens it in triumph though her eyes droop and the muscles quiver. When she stands she is grinning still. The HEALTH VISITOR reddens with relief and satisfaction at her own restraint whilst staging an unconcerned fastening of the lower buttons of her coat. They pause together for a moment, their backs to us, then move slowly around the settee and toward the doors.

HEALTH VISITOR: Another nice cup of tea, Mrs Maule. Always appreciated.

OLD WOMAN: *Nods. A low hum of acknowledgment.*

HEALTH VISITOR: Anything you've forgotten to say to me? Or we haven't talked about yet?

OLD WOMAN: *Silence.*

HEALTH VISITOR: And I suppose you won't let me help with the cups this time either? Eh?

OLD WOMAN: No no. Fine.

This concludes just as they reach the doors and we begin to appreciate the artistry of the HEALTH VISITOR in this professional and crafted leave-taking. It has been tailored for no awkward silences, smoothing her exit for them both. Now she selects the right-hand door of the pair, turns the handle, and pushes to reveal a porch beyond. She steps into this bridge between the inner and outer spaces, reaching. The exterior door opens to an immediate balloon of traffic sound, alarmingly loud, and softer, unidentified scuttling. We can see a flap of sky, too—a thick triangle of afternoon blue. The HEALTH VISITOR stops, acclimatizing, then turns for her farewells, filling the box of porchway and blocking out the slices of external things. The OLD WOMAN stays safe at her end of the runway.

It is time to speak again.

HEALTH VISITOR: I'm away then. Cheerio, Mrs Maule. See you next week. Cheerio then. See and look after yourself now.

If the OLD WOMAN speaks, we cannot hear. With a click and a shudder, the noise cuts and the HEALTH VISITOR is gone, leaving a last cheerio trapped in the silence. The OLD WOMAN closes her interior door and stands motionless. A car horn sounds cheerily outside. The OLD WOMAN continues to face the white door. Her shoulders expand and drop. That is all. When she turns we see the harsh stretch has erased from her mouth and her eyelids are shut. She waits, breathing deeply till the tautness in the room breaks down and settles around her feet; she waits till we feel something has been accomplished. Now we advance.

She begins by clearing the tea things and carrying them off to the room on the right. She nudges the door open enough for us to see inside to a sink, draining board, racks of cleaning materials in bottles. She settles the tray on the stainless drainer, then, with a jerky delicacy that suggests distaste, rinses the cups, saucers and single spoon at the cold tap. As each emerges from the water, she drops it into a red plastic bin at her foot. The dishcloth follows, then, unrinsed, the blue plate and its remaining biscuit. The bin swallows them whole, snaps shut. She wipes her hands against her skirt, reaches and opens the white kitchen unit above the sink. It is scrupulously empty, save in one blushing corner where a red packet flops untidily. The bin accepts this too and the cupboard is clean.

The milk carton is waiting. She takes it from the tray and tips the last of it down the sink, erasing white stains with swirling water. But the determined vigor of her performance begins to tell, for her breathing is audible and she is bracing her arms straight, supporting herself at the edge of the sink. She increases the flow of the tap, masking the sound of her working lungs, but the beating rise and fall of her frail chest seems to worsen. Her head droops, eyes stare: something worming in her throat forces her mouth wide in a retch. The coursing of the water exaggerates deafeningly: we feel the cold scent of steel and the pulsing at her temples—reaching to know what is wrong. Some of us go further. For now the flickering comes again and—single frames of something. Flashing too quickly, a confused mesh of images, unkent things, disconnected pieces.

There is the OLD WOMAN *standing at a full-length mirror in a too-thin nightdress, feeling at her hips through the cloth: now her face at a magnifying mirror, bloated and salivating: a white lavatory bowl darkening with regurgitated matter: a still glass of clear fluid and a clock: a jumble of bones weeping on a bedspread: vomiting.*

But this is revolting. Our empathy snaps back. A thick whiff of nausea, a blink or two, and we are relieved to find the shock has jolted us out of the kitchen and back to our vantage point in the living room. There, reassuringly on the right again, is the OLD WOMAN buttressed at the sink. She recovers in her own time, turns off the tap, straightens her face to the slack-jawed norm. She is coming out—perhaps we should go.

But one door still retains its secret. It radiates whitely from the back of the room. Curiosity makes us stay as she crosses the floor and enters through it, though she closes the blank panel on us almost immediately. A little aural concentration will do: whistling taps, pounding water obligingly reveal an offstage bath. Soon, the sounds of its filling accede to the shuffle of resettling liquid and some coy splashes. Still, it does not do to be too interested; we have learned that from experience. We deflect attention to an idle reexamination of the living room, its pale colors and lightweight furnishings. The diminished rhombus of sunlight on the settee and the carpet shows some time has elapsed. The shifting music of bathing plays from behind the closed door, and, with the monotony of the surroundings, does much to restore serenity. Perhaps we begin to doze. For it is not till the draining gurgle from the bathroom and damp scuffling of the OLD WOMAN's towel that we notice the box, halfway up the wall next to the lamp. At first glance, it passed for a telephone, but now shows a something smaller. There is no receiver. It takes some narrowing of the eyes before we see the switch and the muzzle of an intercom. The box and the surroundings click. This is a sheltered house. Behind this box, in some other place, another living room, is a listener: a caretaker elsewhere, yet securely here in representational plastic. Ah. A little weight drops from our necks.

It is all more containable now, and we can afford a little sentimental soft-focus as she appears at the bathroom door, through a spill of mist in a white dressing gown: an angel in an aura of condensation. Her hair has frizzed out fetchingly with steam and combing, to a frail red and white netting about her skull. Her face is pink, fuller; pretty with rubbing and the heat. And now she moves, her coordination seems easier, as though the invisible bath has oiled the joints to suppleness. More marvellous still are her eyes. Something in the hot-water clouds has freed their color. They are larger, wider: an unnaturally lucid azure. It flashes from under the lids as she turns her head left to right, right to left 180 degrees and back; electric blue pulses from a cardiograph. Satisfied, she crosses the room to the window. She draws the blind, cutting the lifeline of the light shape on the floor and the room relaxes into matching shades of grey. The glare on the wall-mounted photograph, too, drops with a blink, attracting attention. She approaches, looks, touches once. When she turns, we see her rest one fingertip vertically against the flat lines of her lips: *does not equal*. Then, soundlessly, she stretches her hands to the ceiling, fingers in fans, and arms at full reach. They pull away from her till the striving burns: a whimper of pain breaks her concentration. Enough.

Something begins. Some timetable sets in motion with her firm, fluid movements. Her meticulousness suggests planning; preparations made for a specific moment, and, despite our intrusion, the moment is come. She has no need to seize—her grasp is assured. We are too far and at the wrong angle to read her expression with any degree of accuracy, but the set of body, calm manner, and miraculously closed mouth show eagerness, excitement. It seems inappropriate now to cast her as the OLD WOMAN—we must search for another name. Was it . . . yes—it is MRS MAULE. This is MRS MAULE setting her home to rights.

Already, she has moved the armchair away, off to the right. As she rolls aside the settee, a flat, brown packet appears on the carpet in the space it vacates. The center of the room is a newly cleared stage with this single prop. She plumps the settee cushions, erasing the cooled hollow that held her recent guest (now visiting health upon others, elsewhere, with different cup warming her hand) before collecting the rest. First the coffee table, lifted and centered in the thicket of woven flowers, the surface dusted with one cuff. Now, the packet, laid accurately straight along one edge of the tabletop. It is an unremarkable packet, just brown paper with a serrated lip.

To the bathroom next, leaving the door wide. She lifts an orderly pile of fleshy things—the discarded clothes—and drops them into a wicker basket; straightens the bath mat and the towels. There is a small white cabinet above the sink, and two shelves inside ranged with bright bottles, boxes and tins. She pushes her hand among the colors to select a tiny brown jar, then closes the cabinet and the room. They have served their purpose.

Only the kitchen door remains. She wades patiently across and enters, alone. The rattle of a blind, whine of the tap, then she surfaces with a tall glass and a bottle of lemonade. A little awkwardly, she manages to fasten this door too, sealing the interior. The set is ready.

MRS MAULE reaches the coffee table to settle the bottle, glass and pill jar in a neat row along the edge of the bag. She opens the lemonade bottle, then kneels upright behind the table and the row of instruments to fill the glass with sizzling liquid. A pearl string of bubbles, shiny in the half-light, marks a level a few inches from the rim. The rejected bottle sits open on the floor. For a moment or two, she stares

intently at the brown bag before picking it up, gently, with
both hands to spill its filling over the tabletop. A scatter of
paper—several sheets in fresh-to-faded shades of white. One
after the other, she lifts and presses these flat, building a tidy
pile. Each surface spreads in turn under her fingers, some
showing heavily typed faces, some showing nothing. It
takes a little time. MRS MAULE glares hard at her work, her
hands resting on the edges of the sheets. It is difficult to
discern where paper stops and flesh begins, for the light is
very dim now and the blood that quickened in the bath is
slowing, drawing color as it cools. Her face is settling as
she sits, creases returning where warmth leaves. It deepens
as we watch: she is making us wait. Second after second—
almost five minutes. It would be easy to let attention wander, cast around the room, but what is there to see? It is
neat, drab, orderly. All that moves are the silver beads in
the lemonade, shushing a silence from the top of the glass.

It concludes at last. She gathers animation slowly, first opening the pill jar to pour the contents, a straggle of yellow
tablets, across her papers. She discards the bottle and turns
to the glass, raising it in her left hand. The rest is brisk and
decisive. It is a routine. It works like this:

1. A couple of tablets in the right hand;
2. Sip;
3. Insert the pills between the lips;
4. Snap down;
5. Sip;
6. Swallow.

Each cycle ends with a pause, sometimes a curling of the
lip—then begins again. And with greater or lesser pauses,
greater or lesser doses of the yellow tablets, she absorbs the
whole cache. It takes about four minutes in all, not a long

performance, and manages to retain interest throughout. At the end, at least half the lemonade remains in the glass, but the waste is immaterial and she pushes it to one side of the table. Her small weight shifts to one hip, freeing her legs to stretch out in stages. Then, maneuvering lumpily on her elbows, she lowers her back, lying flat on the carpet. She is staring at the ceiling. One hand is restless at her side. It twitches until she accedes to its need. Her gaze does not flinch as she lets it become a thing apart; rising to pluck at the candlewick belt, slipping inside the border of her gown. It fumbles there under the cloth, stroking at one hidden breast. A caress. Soon, she is still again. We notice the crook of her elbow is dry and bulbous: the bath-plumped tissue deflated, unattractively aged once more. Within the waxy face, her eyes keep searching the ceiling. Let her wait on. We have other things to do.

Into the Roots

It was raining and her hair was getting wet. Not a true rain, but a drizzle, layering a blur on individual strands, thickening into fat drops and sliding down to the scalp. She could feel it there already, spreading with the feel of insect feet. Her hair was flattening with the weight, darkening under a dark sky from russet to the vague amberblack of wood resin.

Alice's hair had always been excessive. Even the earliest of her baby photos showed it, wee face struggling out from under heavy cloud. It had been white. She had been told as much and could see in the pictures it was true; hair matching the color of the starched frills under the dazzle of the studio lights. What was not part of a coxcomb strayed out fuzzily as though the child had been plugged into an electric socket or struck by lightning, accounting for the expression of boggle-eyed terror. No matter how hard she looked, it was impossible to detect eyebrows. She supposed they had been white too.

Ash, strawberry, ginger red.
It got darker and it got longer. Through primary school, she carried the weight of its spine-length tangle, brushed,

teased and woven into itself by her mother's efforts of will to a tightbound pleat. Still, it slipped the ribbon to blossom out behind as she ran, shrieking, in the playground.

Evenings had been spent with head bent in contrition at the fireplace, clamped between Mammy's knees as she tore out the knots and condemned them, spitting, to the flames. The longer it got, the more wayward it became. Enough was enough.

She had her first salon cut at the age of eleven: a new uniform and a new persona for the big school. She had been taken by the hand to Carrino's and given up to the dresser— Mammy had other things to do. It crossed Alice's mind she was feart to watch. In the mirror, she saw the familiar coat retreat, open into a square of light, then cut from view as the door clicked across like a shutter. Alice was left gazing at her solitary self and was suddenly, thrillingly aware that this was the last of something. Last snapshot of childhood. She closed her eyes and heard the scissors slice.

Alice had known at the time, had said so, she would never forget the feeling the first incision had induced: as though her head were rising like a cork from the bottom of a sink of water. The dresser gave her the still-writhing pleat to hold: a thick-ended shaving brush petering away to elasticated nothing. She clutched it during the rest of the cutting as someone else emerged in the mirror. A long neck, very white from lack of sun, had grown up in the dark like a silent mushroom. The face was very pale and wee inside a curling auburn crop. They stood her up and dusted off the trimmings then handed her back. Mammy let her keep the pleat and she took it home to put into a shoebox; keeping it to take out every so often and remember who she had been. Then Mammy started calling it *that thing*, brewing a distaste for the precious, matted snake-in-the-box, though when it disappeared no one admitted having thrown it out. It didn't really matter: it was discovered only years later and by that time, the hair was long again.

That first cut triggered fresh growth. So much that within two years its mass had taken Carrino's so long to dress she had been late for the school dance. Slipping embarrassed and hair-sprayed stiff into the squeaky gym-hall with its frenetic Grand Old Duke and illicit kisses. She was never a relaxed child but managed to join in. Enjoyed herself, too: looked well in her home-sewn velvet and starched collar, but she went home alone. People couldn't see her eyes through the fringe and were suspicious. Alice liked it that way.

It brought its penalties, too. She remembered those inter-changeable small boys who had chased and pulled her pig-tail, hoping for a scream that she never gave. Bloodied her lip sometimes, caging in the pain with defiant teeth, deter-mined not to let it show. And there had been a spider trapped in it once, a dark, struggling shape in the red mesh that shook her rigid with fear, numb for what to do. A boy again, this time one with the temerity to approach gently, had come to the rescue. He extricated both the spider and herself into their separate selves again without undue dam-age to either.

She folded her eyelids into a crease. Was it Charles? She supposed it must have been. Fourth year, so it was more than likely. That was the year she had dyed her hair for fun, two separate occasions and two colors, before letting it go its own way without further chemical intervention. The stripes of dye were visible if you looked hard enough, and he must have looked hard to get the spider. Long red step-ladders, falling in fudgy bands of auburn from a straight white center parting to well past her shoulderblades. They had all looked the same. She kept a sixth-year photo: an avenue of senior girls with equiparted skulls and peaky faces aloof to the camera. She was there, right in the front row, fashionably sullen and miniskirted; a leggy bookend with the girl closest. That other girl lived somewhere else now: two weans and no man. That would have wiped the smile off. As for the rest, Alice knew little or nothing; didn't keep up with old acquaintances. It was her mother had done that and it was an easy thing to take for granted when the woman was alive. Just a necessary part of visits home, those tedious chants of births, marriages, turns-up-for-the-books. Scandals. Till she became one herself and moved in with the man, *living in sin* in Charles's flat. Strange now she thought of it. She had never called it hers, for all her work and care there. Always *Charles's flat* or *Charles's* where she had swirled fair beard clippings from the sink, smoothed sheets, sewed neat cushions and learned to cook. She had never noticed at the time and now was too late.

She promised herself a haircut for the week she left—butcher the whole lot short because he had liked it long. But the break had dealt unkindly with her face and the thought of staring it out in a public mirror appalled her. She stayed in instead, putting paper on her own terrifying walls, in a place she would have to learn to call home. She tested smiles in the sheen of a clean bathroom sink, took pleasure from finding single strands of his blond in the weave of her jerseys. Kept finding them too, for a surprising length of time. Though now, sometimes, they weren't real.

Still raining. Misting down now and seeping across her head like melting syrup. Alice was becoming irritable. This was meaningless, merely making it worse. What did she think she was doing out in this weather? Some idea to lift her depression, take a few photographs: the dull metal lump of the camera nuzzled cold into her palm in the folds of her pocket. The others were way on in front. No, it wasn't helping: she was feeling no better and the continual smirr reinforced her suspicion that in walking alone, she was walking with a fool.

The backs of the people on the road ahead grew neither nearer nor farther. One minute, she seemed to be gaining and the next they wavered like slipping frames of cinefilm and were again inexplicably as far as before. Blurred vision—just another side effect to make matters cloudier. Bloody pills. She wondered if she should force herself on, fight the cold denim cloy at her legs and catch up, as though she had fallen behind to tie a shoelace, admire the view. But she deflected the impulse easily. Own company was safest when these moods came.

The decision made her feel much better. Immediately, she stopped walking, stopped trying to make up lost ground and stood still in the middle of the road. Relief rubbed into her shoulders, at the base of her neck, warming affection for the disappearing figures ahead. Let them go.

And this was as it was meant to be. Alice stood and watched the familiar backs retreat as in a mirror. She closed her eyes and heard her heel twist in the gravel of the road; opened them. And there was the broken tree; split and blasted to the sky. Blood rushed to her lips as she smiled. It was a greeting. The tree waited. Alice stepped up onto the banking with one hand stretching and moist eyes. The tree glistened in the rain. Rich red and shrouded in grey. Mushrooming fungus spurted from all its orifices but one and that one she made toward. An eyesocket of a hole, with a swollen lip of bark and moss that only made the wound seem more raw. It would hurt, but had to be done. She steeled the muscles of her arm, flexing with the sound of metal swishing in her ears and cupped one hand ready to receive.

Choking back her fear, Alice thrust out and plunged two clawed fingers into the hole. It was full of hair.

Breaking Through

From the outside you would never have known. People passed in the street and never looked up. All they saw was the boarded-up shop, the empty flat next door, the open close-mouth swallowing in to the dark. But if you went in, feeling through, you saw a square of light high on the end wall, reflecting a shape of itself down on the grey stone steps. The steps had cream edges. They curved and rose to her own front door and opposite, the Sisters' door. The Sisters were very old and indistinct: powdery faces in fur coats, spindly ankles hanging beneath. Their eyes smeared behind thick glasses. They never spoke.

But from outside, there was no hint of the two rooms or their people, perched over the hollow shape that had sold tobacco and sweets, daily news. They were virtually secret.

There was more too.
To reach it, you had to ignore the stone steps and meet the darkness at the flat butt-end of the close. Then you screwed your eyes up tight and there was a brown door with a latch. You lifted the latch and the light spread in a triangle over the paving and you could see, straight in front, the green

hedge like a surprise and the grass. Over your shoulder the car noises, the talk and whistling of people, widening and fading as they passed, and you in the dark with the unsuspected grass and birds and sky. It was better not to wait too long here. Sometimes the wind would come and slam off the blue and green and leave you alone in the deep brown of the close, a stinging hand where the door had been. It was better to slip through and shut the door quickly behind, then turn round and stand in this new place with the garden and the slab path at your feet that took you to Bessie's on the left, the washhouse on the right. Farthest away, the wall that made a boundary of the cemetery. Fingers of obelisks, the tips of tombstones behind the hang of some unidentifiable tree. The two houses, the wall and the hedge made a square and filled it with grass. The brown strips up the sides made Bessie's garden: she had wallflowers. The grass was a drying green and a place for sitting. The Sisters made no claim on it so there was an easy share between Bessie, Janet and her mother. And Blackie. Blackie was Bessie's cat.

Janet visited Bessie at regular times and sometimes other times in between. Most often they sat together in the low front room with a cup of tea each and some biscuits or slices of cake on a plate. Plain cake. Behind their backs, the bedroom that Janet had never seen, at the other side the space with the cupboards and the ring for cooking, the place where you washed cups. The three rooms made a row, like square beads on a string. They were always in the middle of the row, the living room where all the space was filled with big furniture. Bessie would squeeze through with the tea to the chairs at the fire and after that they didn't move. They didn't speak much either. Bessie was not conversational and Janet was shy. Bessie was old with rolled-up hair in a circle round her head and lines on her neck like a tortoise. She was small and thin. Janet was merely six. The attraction in going was not the house or the old woman. The attraction was Blackie. Blackie was lithe and straightforwardly dark till he rolled over. His underside was shock white. Green eyes, pink ears like a rabbit's inside and white whiskers. You could count them. The main thing about Blackie was NOT TO TOUCH. She wanted to touch but didn't. It was good to watch him but better when he rubbed against bare ankles or jumped to make a nest on a carefully stilled lap. That wasn't often. Janet sometimes watched him playing in the garden, and, if Bessie was not there, stroked his warm white underneath as he stretched on the grass. This never eased the wanting though, it was never enough. What Janet wanted was more than that. As though she wanted to feel the essence of the fur, absorb it through the skin till it was wrapped about the bone and part of herself. The want was sore. And the want was always most in Bessie's front room with Blackie on the rug looking into the fire.

Bessie never said much. She was dour her mother said. Terse. This much was a solid, a reassuring nub in their relationship. There had to be something badly wrong then, the day Bessie shouted from the door then rushed up beside her as she played on the grass, arms knitting at nothing, eyes searching for something she couldn't see. Janet knew to follow, fast-moving now the words had stopped, over the grass and brown borders, the weedy slabs to the door and inside, past the cabinet and armchairs.

There was the usual tan color of the fire surround, the ornamental brasses on the mantelpiece. Inside, a black-backed roaring fire. And inside that, framed in flames, the upright vase of the black cat, sizzling in a mound of coals. The fur was catching slowly, jets budding along the dark outline as he sat: front legs taut and tail curled over the paws, head high with the ears in points, their pinkness glinting in the reflected light. Sheathed in golden-hearted arrows of flame, Blackie burned. His eyes were full as green moons.

Something shook her arm. It was Bessie, trying to rouse the child's instinct for action, one to which she herself was lost. Falling on her bare knees, Janet fumbled for the poker at the edge of the tile, raised it then faltered. The cat in the fireplace, the child on the rug: their gaze met and steadied. And Janet knew she would do nothing. She had been taught to respect his privacy too well. It was Bessie who lunged at the coals. The pyre split, caught the inrush of air and blazed higher. A heady, throbbing purr curled suddenly about the room as Blackie seethed, scintillated like a roman candle with the fur searing down and in till all his blackness dazzled out in reds and sparking yellow. The last of him was a flash of green eyes slatted black, a stink of scorched meat. Pork.

Bessie dropped beside the child on the rug. The purring sound had gone and the fire licked tamely in the grate while Bessie sobbed on the hearth, rocking over her knees. Janet put out a tentative hand and held it just above the woman's pulsing shoulder. They were not intimate enough to touch but Janet held her hand there, in the curving space above, till the woman raised herself to face the fire. Her cheeks were quite dry. Though her whole frame shook, there were no tears. Janet allowed herself to relax a little but never took her eyes from Bessie's face. You never knew. Seconds ticked from the mantel clock. Eventually, Bessie clenched her fists and spoke to the open box of the grate: It was what he would have wanted after all.

She closed her eyes and sighed, accepting.
It was settled between the three of them.

It was well after teatime the next day when the girl chose again to slip through the brown door and along Bessie's path with her arm raised to knock. It had seemed the best time: late enough for only a short visit but enough to show she remembered. She waited a moment, concentrating, before letting the tight ball of her knuckles strike. There was no answer. This was not all that unusual: Janet's knock was feeble at the best of times and Bessie was going deaf. Today, it was understandable if both gave in to their weaknesses. She moved away from the door and inched to the front-room window, the hand boned in to her mouth. Inside, in the usual chair, the old lady sat staring into the fireplace. It was the dull twilight time of night or day and the fire was new-built. It existed still as a tumulus of coals with the smoke streaming out between black hollows, twisting together in a spit-color column up the chimney. The underside glittered faintly. Bessie sat deep in her chair, looking.

Janet felt sad and rubbed her fingers lightly on the glass. The old woman didn't see any more than she heard. It would be better to come back later maybe. The girl shuffled over the spongy evening grass, on and across to the wall. There was only the cemetery and a few late birds.

Janet was still looking out counting the tombstones melting against the fog when an echo of her name from a thin mouth reached her shoulder. Bessie was standing at the door, a furrow on the waxy yellow brow, waiting. There was something strange here: not just that Bessie should call out but also that she wasn't properly dressed. She was draped in dark, rose-colored candlewick, held together at the waist with one fist. Her hesitation meant Bessie had to call again and wave the free hand to encourage. She didn't seem angry, just impatient, stepping aside for the child to go inside before she came after. The door closed with a dry squeak of rust.

It was stiflingly hot. The fire had been banked very high and was fully alight now, flashing seesaws onto the wallpaper. Janet stood next to her chair while the old woman faced her. There was something in her hand, held out in an envelope of fingers. It hovered over the space where Janet was expected to open, holding out for whatever was inside. She uncurled her palm and Bessie did the same. A silver-colored ball dropped from one to the other: a split sphere with a bearing inside. A bell. Blackie's bell, cold and whole through the flames. Janet stared for a moment then raised her eyes. They watched each other and the fire crackled. The room was very still, comforting. They touched briefly. Only once.

Bessie stepped back a pace from the rug to let the rose-colored candlewick fall. The child watched her coating of papery skin, limp about the bones and yellowed in the firelight as Bessie stepped up, raising one foot onto the tile surround and nudged the poker aside. Janet kept watching. The old lady steadied herself and breathed deep then in one gliding movement, thrust her body forward into the flames. She managed a half-smile as the child lifted the poker to help.

Fair Ellen and the Wanderer Returned

It was as she rose from stooping, Ellen saw him coming across the grass. Indistinct, with the sun behind him and the big blue sky with the tips of the spruce jagging in. From the bottom of the hill, a line of villagers stared up after him, looking to see what would happen, but it was the man that filled the center of her vision. She saw all this in a single moment, drawing breath, and knew at once.

When he was close enough for her to be able to make out his features, he stopped, staring deep. She was fully erect now, holding the bunch of herbs fresh for the stew. He was trying to smile: she could see him trying. Then he came nearer till he was right in front of her with his blue eyes much as they always had been, but bluer; cracks tracing his brown face where there had been none before. He spoke.

Is it you? his eyes searching.
Ellen
then he fell to his knees, keeling toward her skirt. With both hands he pulled the cloth to his weathered cheek and she felt the weight of it, tugging at her waist as he sank his face into the hemp. She reached slowly to touch his hair, saying

nothing. His hair was thick and greasy under her fingers as he moaned into the dusty cloth.

I have dreamed of this. Dreamed and dreamed of this time, into the rough brown cloth. Her arm that reached to him was spattered with fat from cooking and smelled faintly of garlic. When he stood again, he clasped her elbows in his hands and drew her nearer.

I've come home. As I said I would.
He was breathing heavily and she turned her face a little from the heat of it.
I've come back for you Ellen. We need never be separated again
and he was full with something, his eyes brimming.

All the time as he spoke, she stared with her eyes round, looking into nothing, and when he dragged her close, burying his face into the skin of her neck, she held still and stiff as an ironing board, staring out past his greasy hair to the tops of the spruce trees. He wept and shook against her while the people swarmed at the foot of the hill, peering up yet coming no closer. Something wet touched her, a warm wet suction on the skin of her neck as the man clutched like a garland of need round her shoulders. A kiss. She had almost forgotten the shocking intimacy of such a thing. A kiss.

He drew back then, looking intently into her face. She could see the lines about his eyes and mouth, a snailpath of scar on his brow. The hair that jutted from the skin was shot with grey.

Speak Ellen
but still she did not.

Speak. I've come back. I will never leave again. We can be together now together always.

He shook gently at her shoulders, as though she were asleep and he need only wake her.

Ellen, I've come home.

Yes.
Her first word to him in ten years.
Yes, you've come back. I can see that.

The tears still washing his eyes made them shine like pebbles in the ebb of a rock pool and his smile was full-lipped and tender for her while the scent of the garden herbs, fresh-cut, rose between them.

You have come back as you promised and I'm grateful. But you have come back too late.

She let him stare. It took time till the dullness began filming on his face, seeping slow into his features. She let it take time, then spoke again, knowing he was ready now to hear.

You have come back too late. I am married.

He drew away slowly, still looking as a stiffness moved through his body firming like a wall against the words.

I am married and it will do no good to pretend anything else.
Her face was set and he could do nothing against it so he turned away, sudden and fierce that she should tell him merely what was true and not what he had come to hear.

How—married? Tell me who. Tell me who.
His voice was loud and skirled away to the foot of the hill
where the people still clustered, watching. A show.
Tell me who.
Ellen waited
who?
till his words were quiet as a whisper of leaves on dry grass.

It does no good to be angry. Anger has no future.
She spoke flatly and her face was very hard from having
seen his rage.

What of your promise to me? He spoke for something to
say.

I made no promise. It was you who left. I have always been
here.

He stopped to think, for it was true enough, but he would
not let it be.

I kept my word. I came back. You did not wait for me.
Now I come back to find it has been for nothing. His voice
was rising faster and louder as he loosed the words.
You did not wait.

Then the air between them grew thick. The blood rose in
her face and her eyes glittered black as coal. For a moment,
he thought she might fall from her trembling, then it
stopped, the blood draining back till she was white as death
and just as still. The herbs fell to the muddy grass and she
tilted her head back to the sky, stretching her neck so a
smear of grease rose like a wound at her throat from the
edge of black wool. Then she laughed. Very soft and with
no cheer to the sound, like ash grinding in the grate.

He shifted from foot to foot, unsure. He had been ready to turn away, balanced on one heel to spin from the denials he was sure would come and now the set of his body was wrong: it was no longer fitting. He did not know what she would do and was afraid. Ellen straightened, stiff as before, and crossed her arms over her breasts. She held him in a long, black look.

I waited.
Her voice was full of splinters.
I waited long enough. One year, then another and another I waited while my father sickened and we took on the work of the farm: me and my mother with the sick man to nurse and the land to work and the house to run and I waited. When he died and we sold the stock, I waited as I dragged the plough, fetching and carrying with my hands callusing, waiting in all weathers while I looked out at the sea from the fields. When my mother sickened too and I thought there must be nothing left for us, he came. I turned him away and still he came: an old man with a wedding ring and a promise—a share of money to live. We had nothing and none to give and I turned him away until he asked me, then it was settled. I married him and was dutiful, living through his drudgery and his kindness both till she was dead too. Now he is weak and ill in his turn, an old man who lies in bed while I fetch and carry and grow withered with the years and the waiting. Perhaps he will die soon, but I do not think so.

Her voice was very low and dark. Now it came lower still and the hill was quiet to listen. A bare whisper, yet every word came clear.

And still I was waiting. Something in my heart was watching every day for the sight of you, so I thought it a ghost when you rose finally on the crest of that hill. And now I wish it had been.

Her eyes were hollow.

For now you are here, even hope is lost.

He stared at her, full of bitterness for she had taken away his right to self-pity. He did not know how to answer.

You should go now. Go and not come back.
Yet he waited on, unwilling to give up his dream. He spoke a last hope.

If he should die—
and she cut through his words like a knife across meat.
If he dies I will be free. Look at me. I am grey and cold with waiting. Did you never wonder how it was for me? And do you think now I want to wait again, to fetch and carry for you when your time is come after all these years of nothing? If he dies I will be free for the first time. I have done with waiting.

I loved you. He said it simply and his eyes were dry.

Maybe you did.
Their eyes met and broke.
But it was a long time ago.

He looked at her for a long moment then turned to begin, moving away from this woman in her dowdy hemp and coarse wool. When he reached the rim of the hill, he looked back, blotting the sun.

You're a hard bitch
he said and walked out of sight, careful of every step. She

saw him leave, saw the people scatter as he went down for there had been nothing to see after all.

She stood looking till it grew dark and the shouts of the old man calling for his supper drifted toward her like smoke from the cottage.

Scenes from the
Life No. 24:
Bikers

The bright interior of a chip shop. There is the counter and, beside it, the clean glass case, waiting for the hot fish. Behind the servery, the wall is a multicolor glitter of sweetie jars, spilling forward in ordered ranks of foil-covered bars: chocolate, toffee and boiled sugars. Everything shines, reflecting itself in the hard, grey flooring and Formica.

Set apart are four long tables and eight benches in padded red plastic, blossoming yellow foam at corner cracks. Above, a red clock reads 10:30 unchangingly. There is no queue and not much smell of frying yet.

Someone sits on the table nearest the door, balanced on the linen-effect surface with his legs splayed and the table tip protruding between. It is BIG JIM: a man of about nineteen with a broad build that tends to plump. He wears a recognizable-enough outfit for one who rides or aspires to ride a motorbike: denims faded grainy white at the knees and crotch, an undistinguished blue T-shirt and a charcoal leather jacket. The jacket shows cardboard-colored creases at the joints and its leather is quilted at the elbows and in epaulettes at the shoulders. It is unostentatious, however: no heavy lapels, no collar but a thin mandarin strip with a stud—certainly no badges or mottoes. Fully unzipped, it falls stiffly apart to slide across the front of his body when he moves his free arm. The other is trapped by the fingers in the tight left pocket of his jeans. His shoes are pale beige suede, a smart Italian design and remarkably pristine.

BIG JIM, too, radiates cleanliness. Under neatly cut waves of black hair, the skin of his forehead is luminous, the face clear and florid as though freshly toweled. His temples are babyishly smooth, lips ripe and swollen as fruit; soft ham pinks against the blue cut of his eyes. The single visible hand is thick-fingered coral with nails brushed pearly as the insides of seashells. He seems to smell at once of warm engine oil and cotton, worn leather and talc.

There are two others, sitting next to JIM at the red bench of his table. The skinny ash-blond is angled awkwardly between table edge and the padded backrest, twisting in as though to converse more easily with JIM, though their eyes never meet. The words aim at the other's quilted shoulder or the floor: the content of what is spoken does not seem to determine which.

The third of the group is a bushily ginger-haired man, seated squarely about a foot along the settle from his friends. His elbows stretch wide along the table rim, bowing in to grip a Pyrex cup, gently, in the thumbs and fingertips of both hands. His lips are parted, eyes vacant as he stares at the wall, ignoring the conversation on his left. Occasionally, he peers into the milk film of the coffee cup; nothing more.

It is JIM who does most of the talking. The blond may agree, nod, listen a good deal, but is answering chorus only. It is hard to know where we should break in: they seem so self-sufficient and give so few clues. It may as well be now.

Butterfly valves.

Jammed. Like constant choke eh.

He makes a sucking sound as though drawing on a cigarette.

Gap too wide. Corroded head mibby. Check the spark.

Already it is reassuring. No matter how much of the exchange we have missed we have lost nothing, for this is not narrative. It is a cyclic discussion where any starting point is as good as the last for everything will be repeated sooner or later. Mechanical hypochrondria.

Aye. Butterfly valves right enough.

Insulator OK.

They chant in minimalist verses, machine-shop precise to make patterns of tappets and points and overheated coils; they cite the intimacies of decoking, gumming and greasing and, though their intonation never changes, their eyes shine. A ritual by heart: components of tea-ceremony delicacy for Zen brothers in black leather robes.

But we are getting carried away. BIG JIM seems to have paused for thought while our attention has been elsewhere and the mood has altered. His brow has darkened and when he speaks now it is no longer poetry: it is far too comprehensible.

Told him but. They canny prove it. Canny prove nothing. Canny make him. Might no even be his. Canny be sure.

JIM and the blond are staring at the same square of lino, as though something is appearing on its surface through the floor. JIM's eyebrows rise in disbelief.

Mind that lassie two year ago.
Big Cass would've married her as well. Settled—had it her own way. No problem. Jumped in front of a lorry. Mill Road corner.
All over the road eh, all over the road. Still see the skids.

Bloody daft. He was gonny marry her as well.

BIG JIM relaxes his gaze, clouding his eyes to let them settle more placidly under the lids once more.

Canny touch Jazzer though. Canny prove it. No even his, but.
Me an Beejay helping him wi the matchless later on. Still in bits. Off the road a month already.
Terrible.

Neither the blond nor the redhead respond. JIM waits for a moment before rising from the table, creaking. The blond calls after as he reaches the door.

Checked the circuits last night. Fine.

JIM turns.

Clogged jets.

A sudden spiteful hiss of hot fat announces the owner, setting about his day's work scalding the first batch of chips.

The place is immediately cheerier. They raise their voices to arrange things. Jazzer, Cass, Beejay, Spazz and Big Jim: they will gather at the Mill Road Corner with their bikes revving for greeting, repeat the day's business and cheer up an old friend. They smile at each other with the promise of their meeting. Later, there will be no digression. Their minds will be clean, prayers for gods that will one day run smooth as silk, purr like kittens, ride like dreams.

Need for Restraint

suddenly
they were both on the ground clutching up
gouging and hacking with hands pulling at cloth and
snatches of hair wound on fingers the flat of flesh slapping
dull on tile

THERE IS NO REASON FOR THIS

She stood looking while the men made their terrifying vi-
olence inside the muzak of the shopping mall. Runnels of
people practicing mass avoidance kept to the other side of
the walkway. A man in a suit skipped over a wrist and kept
going, just kept going. Then there was a click off the paving
and a crunch like bone jesuschrist and dark hair splashing
out, the thud of soft bodies through the soles of these shoes.

THIS IS NOTHING TO DO WITH YOU

But somebody had to do something. She felt her mouth
hang slack. People were stopping. They were looking.
Somebody should do something.

A hand.

She watched as it moved, a hand stretching. Those thin
white fingers. Her own hand reaching for one of their shoulders. And she thought she spoke. Somebody will get hurt.
It was a thin testing voice she heard. Her mouth felt hardly
used and the shoulder in front was melting under her palm
as though neither she nor the voice were there. But she was
there. An elbow clipped her knee and made it sure. She was.
People were looking.

Somebody will get hurt if you don't stop it.
The dark man stopped, his fist raised. He looked round.
Somebody's supposed to get hurt, that's the fuckin idea.

Of course. The obviousness of the thing made her dizzy
and hot with her own stupidity. It made her not able to
think so the action, when it came, was instinctive. It was
beyond her control. Her hand thrust forward, reaching for
the stranger's face. She watched her fingers stroke his cheek,
the light burr of stubble on the tips. One clean kiss of skin
where nothing moved or sounded, and dreadfully out of
place. The man's arms flailed toward her, jerking backward
as though she had scalded him, his face twisted. He steadied
himself, staring with his eyes narrow and just as she thought
he might hit her, looked quickly aside. Alert. The other
man was struggling to his knees, preparing. It was going
to resume. Then a pair of hands, rough, grainy hands flapped
like wings into their tightening space. Not for her. They
came to make way for information.

Enough boys.
The men hesitated.
Enough. That's enough. Break it up eh.

Another voice, weaker than the first, backed up the same. Aye enough boys godsakes.

And it was. There was some grudging dusting down, some hard looks but no more words, no fighting. They had known what to do and say, these men. She had not. People were moving about again, breaking and slipping into the mass and leaving her standing. She felt clumsy, inept. Female. Within seconds it would be impossible to tell those who had seen from those who had not. It wouldn't matter. None of it would matter. Walk. She should walk.

THIS IS NOTHING TO DO WITH YOU

and the supermarket was just at the end of the mall. Hardly any distance. She began to walk then, stickily, watching the neon expand, the letters grow. The sheen on the windows faded when she got close. Inside was full of people, checkout queues and girls in loose pinafores stacking boxes. The face floating between them was herself, a reflection off the glass wall. She looked down, scowling at her hands. They were trembling.

BUT THERE WAS NO REASON
this overwhelming nothing of a thought
NO REASON

Her stomach tightened as she looked up. The white glass face would still be there. It was important not to see it, to try to remember.
She was WHERE
outside the supermarket. Here with her back to the fountain in the precinct and she was WHAT WAS IT
waiting for Charles. She was meeting Charles here at the fountain: Friday ritual of shopping at the end of the week

then take the bags home in Charles's car. That was it. She was meeting Charles. WHEN
at five.

Five.

Christ it was past that now. Her eyes flicked from the watch-face and he was there: Charles in the doorway of the chemist opposite. He was looking in, investing crêpe bandages and tubes of lubricant with significance to kill the time. Alice felt her shoulders relax. She knew who she was when she saw him there. She was Alice because he was Charles, her man. He was waiting for her. There was no telling from the set of his face that he hadn't been checking his watch, building a grudge at having to wait in this public place. He kept looking in the shopfront, not knowing she was there. The usual relief, the usual anxiety. She was in no mood for blame but she was also late. There wasn't time to work out tactics. Not now. Breathing deep, hoping for the best, Alice crossed to meet him.

Routine found its feet the moment he saw her. There was the usual touchless greeting, smiles no greater or less than they always were. Already they were exchanging nothings about the working day: already the word *fine* had been over-used satisfactorily. As she was forming it again, Alice knew very clearly this wasn't what she wanted. This wasn't it at all. She wanted something at the corners of her mouth to tug out of shape; wanted him to see and ask what was wrong. She wanted him to notice. The smile was stuck and she let it stay there, getting maskish and ugly, seeing him look and not look. His eyes swerved, deliberately finding the fountain, staring it out. That cold set of his jaw and the sigh. Soon the smalltalk would get stiff: bitty and challeng-ing. Applying a course of correction while he refused to look her in the eye. He would not ask. She would not ask him to. If she persisted, there would be silences, an uncompanionable coldness as they trailed the supermarket shelves. He would turn that self-sufficient way, keep himself clammed and tight into the evening. It could go on like that for days. She knew all this. She knew it wouldn't make any difference. But she wasn't able to stop. The need to speak was terrible now. Saying, saying anything, might loosen this lump in her chest. This time, she'd keep it light, not whine at least. If they laughed it would be better.

Something funny. Something funny just—
He had focused past her. He was looking into a place behind where she was, making her an obstruction to his clear view.
I don't feel very well.
This was at least true.
Oh, he said.
People were looking. She had to go on, making this messy account in disconnected fragments.
Two men. Two men started fighting. In front of me when I was coming to meet you just now. Just over nothing. No reason for it and nobody did anything, they just stood and—
What did you expect them to do?
He knew though he asked. He asked what had to come.
And I tried to stop them. I said someone will get hurt and one of them, one of them—
She was hot, sweating because she knew she was making it worse and not better and she couldn't seem to stop. She knew she should know better. And he knew too. He could hardly keep his head upright.
Her voice was out of shape
and one of them said that's the fucking—
DON'T SWEAR
A vitriolic stage whisper so expected she wondered if he

had spoken at all or if she had made the sound from her
own fear.
—and he looked at me as if

But Charles knew exactly how the man had looked at her.
The words jammed. They stopped. Something wormed in
her throat and her eyes were filling up. Charles shook his
head. Between anger and despair, he hissed: christ there are
people looking.

There was the dull thump of his fist against glass. Alice
knew he had turned his back. Soon, he would walk away
into the shopping mass and leave her to go home alone. She
had not even said what she wanted to say. Feet clattering
at the fringes of her vision hurt, a soreness in the temples
as she stared down at the tile. Its red color was blurring
now, melting. Something was playing, uninvited, on the
backs of her eyes.

It had been a dark evening through long windows. Thick
royal sky and a luminous part of a moon and the street
beyond the glass in cast-off bronze from the sodium lights.
Grass on the verges grey and orange. Then the shouting:
drunken loudmouthing as the men rounded the corner and
the shapes and the noise of them pushing and shoving. Like
animations on a screen. Then the change: something quick
and one of them rocking forward, calling out. A sheen. It
was something shiny. Her mouth flexing, realizing a knife
and the three men tangling and dissolving in the half-light,
the shouting changing to something metallic. Blood. And
seeing that, her chest rippling with wakefulness and that
terrible need to do something, thinking of the blood. She
remembered reaching the door and being full of breath,

pushing. But it was not wood or glass beneath her hand: she was pushing at warm cloth. Warm cloth filled with flesh so she looked up and it was Charles. Charles blocking the way with his eyes very blue, the voice calm with his information: it was

NOTHING TO DO WITH YOU
NOTHING TO DO WITH YOU
NOTHING TO DO WITH

buzzing through his chest and into her palms and the screaming rising outside while she pushed again, needing to break free and go. And suddenly his voice changing, hard as the grip on her wrists, repeating while he held her still: it was NOTHING TO DO WITH YOU and she was GOING NOWHERE and NOT INVOLVED; louder and angrier if she struggled.
NOTHING TO DO WITH YOU
NO REASON FOR THIS

And it was then she felt hate boiling like gas through the veins, up and through the skin like branding. There was no reason between them. No reason. The street and the men were just something outside and far away. Everything was here, inside the room with this man and this woman, she in his arms and shaking with rage till he was holding her tight. Holding her. She stopped twisting, looking down and he looked too. He was holding her. Their shapes cut against the black night-glass of the window: a man and a woman embracing in a room. Alice and Charles and this fearful, ringing nothing. He let her go quickly and covered his face with his hands. They stayed apart for the rest of the night, ignoring the street outside and the faint cries rising over distant roofs, the drips of blood on the pavement. They did not mention it again.

. . .

A scraping of heels like chalk on slate came too loud. There were the tiles of the precinct, rush-hour shoes. It wasn't right that this be here. She was at fault somehow. To have seen so private a thing before so many strangers, these indifferent shelves, boxes of liniment. But he was still turned away and it was impossible to speak. He flexed, his coat steeling. To speak would only make things worse. Yet if she touched him now, he would go without her. That might be kind. It would be something. Deliberately, she reached, tipped the warm cloth of his coat. He broke free as she knew he would, moving to merge with the crowd.

People were looking. People were looking.

Plastering the Cracks

It was more serious than I at first supposed. Not that I hadn't known the place needed attention. I knew all right: there was a lot to do and I was quite confident I would manage. For the most part, I was right. But when I started in that back room, peeling back that first strip of bedroom paper, the issue became more complex. Plaster clung and came away with the paper, leaving soft craters in the wall, pouring little rivers of silt when I touched them. It was regrettable but obvious I would need help. I tore down the rest of the paper anyway, letting more plaster drop and lie among the cast-off bits. If I had to hire someone, the room was going to look its worst. I wanted my money's worth.

I researched the *Home Handyman Encyclopaedia* that night. There wasn't much in the way of advice but I managed to find some information about structural damage and that made me feel a bit better. I could drop in some background knowledge, sound informed so they wouldn't try and fast-talk me or bump up the cost. The services page in the local paper had plenty of small ads, all different. I scanned each in turn and chose two plain minimalist efforts, ringing them heavily with black Biro.

The call box at the end of the street was working and I got through first try. Arrangements were polite and brief: both could come round to estimate next morning within half an hour of each other. The whole business had taken less than five minutes to set up—smooth as silk. I made a few calculations in my head on the way back: a couple of days for the plastering, maybe another fortnight for my work on the rest of the house, then move the furniture in. It could be done no bother. I penciled the notes into my jotter when I got in and poured myself a whisky. I read the *Home Handyman* till it was too dark.

Next morning, I didn't need the alarm. I was up and shopping for warm rolls and a morning paper before seven. Two jumps ahead. The first man was at the door by eight.

He was thin and dark, belonging to the more detailed of the two ads. His inspection of the bedroom unaided took six minutes. He was chatty but pretty po-faced. I had to understand it was more than just plastering the cracks. The whole room would need to be stripped down and resurfaced, some floor panels replaced and the old fireplace could be knocked away. Did I know there was rising damp too. He could do the lot for a fixed price of two hundred pounds and begin in a fortnight. When I didn't say anything he told me to think it over. Phone in a few days, check the estimate; let him know. He let himself out.

The next one came twenty minutes later. He had a red face, not much breath and an overtight shirt. His trousers sagged. A woollen bunnet jammed too far down his brow made it hard to see his eyes and I lost concentration on what he was saying till I realized he had stopped. Then I took him through. He went in gingerly, padding at the walls. I was going to leave him to it, then something hooted behind me and I wheeled back. He was facing me directly, too close. The face under the bunnet was rawer in the pale light, his clothes dustier. Another hoot and a rumble, then the fists gesturing near my face. He was explaining something but I couldn't catch it. Just couldn't get the drift at all. It was as though he had a terrible speech defect and no teeth. He kept going through, repeating the same things a few times and miming with his hands. I got the gist it was an estimate. I repeated it: he could do the plasterwork and brick the fireplace for fifty pounds. That wasn't it. I had got it wrong: he held up three fingers, sighed and wrote in pencil on the wall, thirty pounds. He could do the work for *thirty pounds* and start as soon as I liked. I asked him to start next morning, and a smile spread under the hat as I shook his hand, a huge hand with hair all the way down to the nail. My own disappeared inside it. I went with him to the back door and gave him a key in case I was out when he arrived, then waited, waving, till he was out of sight round the corner. That was it. I was pleased with the morning's business. I had thought of everything, hired someone to work for me at knock-down rates: I could handle things. I was nobody's fool. Nobody's mug.

Sometime after 11:30 next morning, he arrived. I heard the word LATE as I let him in, but couldn't recall having specified a time and said nothing. In any case, he had already begun shuttling between a blue van outside and the bedroom, filling the place with stuff; floury sacks, plastic bins, canvas bags, big polythene pokes full of grey powder; tins of putties, cans, small foil-covered squares and fattily transparent paper bags. I watched from the corner of an eye. On the fourth or fifth journey, he went into the room and reappeared simultaneously at the back door. The second self had the sun behind it, and was smaller and thinner. When it came down the lobby it was another man altogether. I was a bit shaken anyway, and went back to fitting the carpet.

It wasn't long till I started enjoying myself. I liked cutting the hemp, the awkwardnesses and angles of the room. I had a new ruler. As I worked, soft shuffles on the other side of the wall increased my concentration. Grating whispers. Stone, sand, knuckles on board: a cushion of low, male voices. There were two of them now, bridging the space between our separate rooms with muffled somethings. Wool and foam parting roughly under the Stanley knife, human warmth seeping beneath the skirting.

Shortly after one, I went out for a hot pie and a doughnut from the bakery. The cooker wasn't fitted yet and besides, I liked going there for the savory scent of it and the heat. I was going to spoil myself since I'd finished the carpet. An overturned cardboard box did for a table and the bakery bags for plates. Even so, the feel of the place still wasn't right. I could hear myself too plainly, moving about, and realized what I was missing was the company. I got out the radio and turned on whatever there was to fill the space. I started to wonder if they were eating, too. Maybe they were eating just as I was, hearing my radio. Maybe they liked the sound of me through the wall as much as I had enjoyed them.

Now there was nothing at all. The last part of the grey meat went cold in my fingers as I listened for them listening. When I noticed, I threw it in with the carpet offcuts and slithered the grease off down the sides of my jeans: I'd have a bath later. I could induce no interest in the doughnut and put it back inside the bags: it would keep. I turned the radio down and slid a fresh blade into the yellow Stanley handle.

KETL
A word and a sound like a tearing sheet made me turn abruptly.
KETLHEN IH

The fat man crammed the living-room doorway. I had heard nothing of his approach and here he was right inside the room, speaking. He sipped self-consciously from an invisible cup to help me with the words. KETTLE. ONY TEA.

I got up and backed him down the lobby, gesticulating into the space behind him as I walked forward. Once we got to the kitchen, I pointed out the kettle and ran the cold water too hard to demonstrate his welcome to it. The wool bobble nodded. Mushrooms of hairy flesh popped between his shirt buttons as he moved. Under a thick lip of fat, settled on the waistband, his trouser catch was open. I flicked my gaze away quickly but he was happy at the taps and hadn't seen me looking so I slipped back out. Back down the tunnel of hallway, into the brightness behind the living-room door. Snug crush of nylon pile under my knees, I was absorbed for the rest of the afternoon, wiring.

At 4:30, a muffled shout hurled up the lobby and the bobble hat pushed round the door.

ATSUZ THIDAY
He filled his lungs heavily several times while I said nothing.
BACK THIMORRA OKAY
SOKAY HEN
he insisted as I tried to get up, a good-natured dismissal as he saw himself out. Irritation at my own cluelessness hung on through the diminishing sound of feet. I hadn't been able to hear him right. No, *that wasn't it.* I had heard perfectly well. It was more that I didn't seem able to get to the bottom of what he was saying. I couldn't work out a meaning. It reminded me of a habit I got into as a child, something that passed the time on long bus journeys. I would let the engine noise sink me into a kind of hypnosis till the sound lost its

significance. Then when people spoke, their words became simply noise, disembodied from sense. Conversation became at once incomprehensibly foreign and deeply soothing; threatless music to block out exteriors. I could switch it on at will. I encouraged it. But when it began to affect me unbidden I was frightened and stopped the practice by sheer effort of will. Now, a shadow of that fear crept into the bare living room and up my neck, till a sudden raucous farting from the street chased me to the window. An ancient exhaust on the carcass of a blue van. I clutched the sill and watched it pass; T. G. BOYD BUILDER and a snatch of bobble hat.

I was painting when they let themselves in, calling their arrival down the hall. The fat man flooded the doorframe. MAKE TEA FIRST EH. It was quite clear, I heard him fine. There was also a promise of self-containment about it that let me off having to make silly small talk. Gratefully, I shouted through for him to take some rolls if he liked, and soon after, heard them in gentle manly belches of appreciation through our wall. I thought of them in there, in my bedroom, eating buttered gifts with hot tea.

By lunchtime I had the makings of a headache. The narrow windowframe needed a great deal of concentration and I had already smeared the glass twice. Maybe I needed my dinner. It would be nice to be out for a wee bit of fresh air too, away from the paint fumes. Only a short walk to the bakery, but it would do.

I selected a sausage roll and an empire biscuit. The woman touched my hand giving me change and called me dear. I was feeling better already. The lobby was thick with dust when I got back; enough to make the air visible. Dull thuds from the bedroom confirmed they had started on the heavier stuff, knocking away the brickwork or something. While I made my tea, the thumping got worse. There was no milk. I looked around a bit before realizing it was likely in with them—in the bedroom with their morning tea things, but I wasn't going to interrupt their concentration or my privacy to collect it; it wasn't that important. I settled for black and walked back through chalky clouds, roaring like dry ice under the door.

I enjoyed the food. I'm sure I did. After all, I had been painting all morning and I was hungry. But I was increasingly aware of the headache all the time I was eating. I thought it was most likely the noise from the back room that was doing it, or the hangover of turps. I rubbed my temples as another crash like rockfall billowed through the wall, followed by muttering and laughter: I clearly heard the word STARVIN and others less distinct. I picked up my brush when it stopped.

It was a long afternoon. The window smudged to spite me and I got fed up wanting it done nicely in favor of merely getting the thing finished. My eyes frazzled as the paint wiggled off the brush-end like white insects. I was still at it when I heard them packing up to leave. That time already. I took their tip, waited till they had gone for sure then wandered up the lobby. Some tea, maybe, and yesterday's doughnut to keep me ticking over. A wee doughnut would do me fine.

It wasn't there. I checked all the likely places and a few of the more bizarre. I knew I hadn't thrown it out and I knew I hadn't eaten it either. I caught a glimpse of the bag near the sink. Its whiteness hurt as I picked it up and I had to peer to make out some thin pencil scrawl written on the lower edge. It was a message. THANKS FOR THE DOG-

NUT. T.G.'s writing. He must have assumed it had been part of a lot with the rolls. Then I remembered about the milk; it would still be through there as well. Right. I would collect it now. It was time I checked up on what they had been doing in there anyway. It had been two days after all, and it couldn't be far from finished. Hadn't even expected them to stay this long, not for thirty pounds. Not for thirty pounds for two of them. Christ. I could hear my head fizzing like Alka-Seltzer. What if the estimate had been partial or something? for materials only, and labor was extra? What if I hadn't understood? I rushed down the lobby, then pulled up stiffly at the closed face of the bedroom door. I took two deep breaths. Then I twisted the handle and walked unflinchingly inside.

Inside.

It was light and dark at the same time and the walls were moving. They were sliding and changing color in huge suppurating spots. In the middle of the textured ceiling there was a glittering ball of mirror chips, rotating and sparking out light that turned on the wall in formless, spreading blobs. For a while, I was too taken in with this to see much else. It was only with much effort I managed some furtive glimpses of the rest of the room. There were long poles in one dim corner, leaning like clothes props, and tool sacks, pregnant with hidden lumps. Bottles of dark fluids, metal bars, cups of powder. Near the blinded window, a huge sofa, piles of magazines, empty cans. And the remains of my doughnut. Around and under everything, the floorboards were still bare, the walls still meshed with soft cracks. I couldn't see what they had been doing to the fireplace since it was masked with an old-fashioned fire screen, heavily embroidered with leering birds of paradise and peacocks whose eyes glowed and receded in the colored rays from the ceiling.

And there was the milk, inches away, near my foot.

Seeing it there restored some of my equilibrium. Just a green and white carton with dark brown lettering and a cartoon drawing of a cow relaxing on a milkstool. I fixed my eye on the smile of the cow, trusting it to keep the rest at bay. For the rest—I knew even as I was watching—the rest was not really there. It was ridiculous. If I ignored it, it would go away. My head pounded as I stooped to pick up the carton and walked backward out of the room, keeping my breath steady till I got out. Then I pulled the door shut too hard and loosened more plaster. I could hear it scratching against the boards inside. Too bad. I had to stop it spreading to the rest of the house, keep it under control. Then I knew that was daft. My own overactive imagination. I wanted to smile. HA HA I laughed up the hall; HA HA along the tunnel into the dark. Time I had that tea and a bit of a rest. Yes, a nice cup of tea then I would relax for the night. My mind was made up to forget the whole thing till the next morning. Yet I tiptoed to the bathroom and moved the sleeping bag round on the floor before I went to sleep. Better safe.

Accordion music. Accordion music woke me. I sat up still inside the sleeping bag to listen. There was a rhythmic swishing noise as well, and both were coming from very near. They were coming from the bedroom. I heard a clear single word: HOOCH—and some undistinguished guffaw- ing. I checked the alarm. It was well after ten. I had overslept and they had let themselves in, had started work in the back room. Then I wondered if they had come up the lobby as usual, opened my door, looked in on me when I was asleep. Maybe spoken about me, laughed about me when I couldn't hear. I was irritated, embarrassed and confused. I didn't want to go to the bathroom if they were in the hall either.

The easy way out would be to go across the road—wash and breakfast in the bakery coffee bar and give myself time to come to. I would think of something then. Laughter welled up behind me as I slammed the front door.

It worked, though. By the time I returned. I felt much brighter. I made a lot of noise with the front door so they would hear. I had worked out a plan as I sat in the shop and knew exactly what I was doing. It was time I pulled myself together and started moving around my own home as though it was my own home. They would walk all over me if I didn't.

I strode purposefully across the carpet and down the lobby, then stopped at the bedroom door to listen for my moment. They were talking. The words SOON and OKAY came through the accordion tunes, then T.G.'s voice cut clear, making perfect sense NO BE LONG NOO and sighing.

It took the wind out of my sails. If everything was well in hand, there would be no need to get heavy-handed. They seemed to be gathering stuff together. I slipped away into the kitchen. The first thing I saw was the milk carton. A fresh one. They had brought me a new pint.
AYE. NEARLY BY. DO WIYA BATH EH. I kept the voices in my ears and picked up the carton, holding it to my chest. Things were all right. Everything was under control. T.G. began to sing tunelessly in a light baritone.

I didn't need the tea but I made it anyway and went to sit with it in the living room and check the list I had written.

1. SORT OUT BUSINESS—SEE ROOM!
2. HOW MUCH LONGER?
3. Second coat on interior door.

I scored out 1 and 2, ringing 3 with a flourish, then switched
on the radio for the shipping forecast. I was almost relaxed.

The door proved easy after yesterday's windowframe. Paint
rolled off the brush in merging strips while people talked
about gardens on the radio. When it got boring, I switched
off and went on with the paint. So I didn't notice the silence
at first. But it thickened as time passed and I soon checked
my watch. After two. That meant no sound at all from next
door for well over three hours. They couldn't have gone
already because I hadn't paid anything. And the van was
still there on the other side of the road: T. G. BROWN murky
under the filth. I moved quietly to the bedroom door. Nothing. I tapped at the closed panels, listening hard. Then something bubbled suddenly behind me, the plumbing groaned.
Instinctively, I propelled myself forward away from the
noise and into the room.
I should have known.

There was a deck chair in primary stripes right in the center
of the bare boards. Crushed beer cans and two billiard cues
made a pyre in the corner near a crude newsprint pinup.
Another corner glinted with dustless tools, polished chrome
and steel. Breathlessly, I scanned for evidence of their labors.
The cracks on the wall nearest me had peeling oblongs of
sellotape over their mouths; those higher up seemed completely untouched. An old piece of skirting had been reat-
tached with orange Plasticine, bulges of it oozing between
the wood and the wall. Some stone had been chipped off
the fireplace and lay in a heap where the surround had been.
The grate was full of crumpled bits of the *Daily Record*,
strapped in place by a mesh of masking tape. The bubbling
noise rose up again, more identifiable this time. The rush
and whinny of water. It was coming from the bathroom.
Splashing and muted giggling. T.G.'s unmistakable enun-

ciation: SOAP. Then I saw: penciled on the grubby plaster round the lightswitch, a scribble of naughts and crosses and some words. APRIL FOOL. Water rushed in the bathroom. The bastards were having a bath.

Furious, I lunged for the living room and hunted out some paper. I forked the pen out from under the tool box then sat to write.

OUR CONTRACT IS TERMINATED FORTHWITH. PLEASE COLLECT YOUR STUFF AND LEAVE.

Then I fished out the three ten-pound notes I had kept in my purse from their first day, waiting for them. Too bad if I had got it wrong: it was all they were getting. I put them with the letter into a manila envelope, sealed it, stormed down the hall and unhesitatingly stuffed the lot under the bathroom door. The sound of toweling stopped abruptly. There was a dry click of paper as a fat hand found the envelope. That was enough. Blazing with trepidation and triumph, I left the house and walked as fast as I could to the bus stop.

All the streetlights were burning when I got back. The van was gone: I had seen that much as I walked up the street. I called out at the back door to make sure: COOEEE. But nothing answered. The kitchen was very dark inside, darker even than the road, but I waited till I got used to it and found I could see pretty well without putting the light on. I preferred it that way. I would have a wee look in, then plan for tomorrow; check out what had to be done in there and work out how to do it myself.
Fresh start. I had my *Home Handyman*, my notebook. I would manage.

The doors gaped in a Russian doll series behind me as I made through to the bedroom. It was open, and the blind for once was up. I looked.

The walls were smooth, the fireplace bricked and flat. The drying plaster had been sanded and a heap of plaster dust smoked in the corner near my kitchen brush. On the white windowsill, outlined in moonlight, were some bits of paper and something silver. The spare key, a dull, crushed oncer and a note from T.G.

CHANGE.

later he would open his eyes in a strange place, wondering where she

They'd planned it for his sixty-fourth birthday, her having been retired a few years now and his redundancy money spent. Thursday: the day the mobile library came round. She had handed him the book with the bit underlined, in pencil so she could rub it out before she took it back: just the bit that mattered. He thought at first it was something to do with her amateur theatricals that she'd done for years up till the bad hip meant she couldn't get out and about as much, but it wasn't that. It was something different altogether. Maybe if she hadn't liked biography. Koestler. She remembered it because she didn't know how you said it, how the sound of the word went. Even if she'd gone to another shelf. It was his ticket that got the book out, him not being a reader. She pointed that out. He looked at it eating toast and didn't say yes or no just nodded: he had heartburn. But two nights later he put the book on the mantelpiece while she was looking at the TV. It was closed but she looked up anyway, knowing, with the look on his

face saying he'd been thinking. And he knew from her looking up, watching his face like that, it would be his respon-
sibility. They said nothing else. She went back to watching
the chat-show host talking to people she'd never heard of,
listening to the creak of the stairs under his weight, quieter
with every footfall.

It was probably the night she said she'd a notion of ice cream,
eaten nothing all day but had a notion of ice cream and
nearly eleven o'clock with the cafés and everything shut it
took shape. He had taken the car rather than walk to find
somewhere because you never knew in those precincts late
at night, the screaming and so on. With them not going for
the Sunday drives anymore it would be something for the
car to do, open the engine up. It gave him a fancy for a
drive, just round the ring road and back, past the digging.
There were always cones these days, right along the edge
of the road or making islands in the middle. They were
building a wall. He slowed down a bit to look at it, nearly
finished. End to end as long as the fencing that had been
round where the steelworks used to be. Just bricks. Maybe
they would plaster it over to make it look better later on,
put one of those murals on it. A mural of the steelworks.
His hands felt dry, coated with dust, feeling for the absent
plaster.

The only place this far out was the Little Chef. It was bright
anyway. He had a cup of coffee, sitting in with four men
eating and a pair of girls with black hair and white faces,
even their lips powdered over and black rings round their
eyes like bruises. The place was full of some music you
couldn't quite identify or hear properly. He sat with the
coffee, trying not to watch the other people too much and
listening to this terrible distant music till a girl with a mob-
cap came and tried to refill his cup that wasn't empty. You

couldn't finish the coffee in these places. Halfway out the door he remembered about the ice cream, about the whole point. She would be wondering where he was and Pieroni's would be shut. He had to go back inside, letting the door swing hard behind him.

There was ice cream in the chest freezer next to the computer game machines. He'd have to take something with being away ages. No vanilla, only chocolate cone things and blocks of stuff with flavors. Maple and pecan nut. She had a sweet tooth. He paid the money and left with the ice cream burning his hand through the paper bag. On the way back, he noticed the petrol light, orange dot on the dashboard as he was approaching the wall and the flat stretch at the old steelworks but he kept his foot down. He didn't want to double back now. Then, for no reason he could think of, he remembered the book. The book. He watched the wall in the rearview mirror, big wrapper of it round the derelict space getting smaller. She was fine about the ice cream when he got back. He made her a cup of tea to take up and sat on downstairs thinking. He thought all night. It was a change to have something to think about. Neither of them slept much these days anyway.

Not the next morning but a couple of days or so after he said. Waiting for her to bring the breakfast. She didn't even look up, just tipped the egg on his plate: always a whole egg though he only ate half these days what with not being able to taste much and the texture sometimes making him feel sick. Then she stood, waiting for the plate as usual, the half white and yolk oozing over the hairline crack on the blue painted lip. There was nothing ostensible. But when she was pouring the tea, he felt a stiffness between her arm and his shoulder, something different in the space over his head. When she sat down he saw her eyes had filled up so he knew she had heard. She didn't always hear. Next morning he could tell she'd been thinking about it too. She suggested the paraffin. A refinement.

Preparation was minimal. She looked out the marriage lines and the two policies while he went to the filling station. He came back with a full tank and a bar of chocolate, the kind she liked, out of habit but she didn't smile. She was worried about the house.

I know but I can't help it.

He couldn't think of anything to say, just waited, clinking keys, watching her manage the sleeves of the pink tweed coat she bought cut-price and never liked, folding the paisley scarf. She had to push the plastic flowers in front of the cracked bit of mirror to put on lipstick. He wondered about getting his hat then didn't because she was turning toward him, looking anxious, pressing the stud at the coat collar. It wouldn't shut. She gave up and looked round.

Nothing else?

The plastic bottle with the paraffin was already in the car from the morning. There was nothing else. But neither moved to the door. There was a tug of something there, something between them like an invisible mesh of threads, the possibility of embrace. When she looked away, it broke. They left the chocolate on the sideboard, unopened. The car started first turn, without shuddering.

Life in the old girl yet, he said. The smell of petrol from the leaky tank was overpowering.

Now there would be the drive across the bridge and into the wasteland by the steelworks wall, the wait in the sickly upholstery smell with the handbrake on hard, the car ticking over like a child's cough. Ticking over and lurching as though it might stall, the way it did these days, so you could never wait too long, the car not suited to idling. They would avoid the other's touch as they turned in the tight space, when she reached into the back to find the plastic bottle, moving to pour the paraffin, keeping dousing till it was all gone and the fumes making her turn to roll down the window before she remembered not to. The windows would need to be shut. Almost a joke. Then the engine revving back from the brink of a cough, his hand jerking and relaxing on the lever, the car beginning to roll. And he would tilt the tires over the crest of the mud hill, set the wall in his sights and drive, accelerating till the engine whines and the bodywork trembles, her hands blue-veined on the dashboard, holding the ledge tight.

Life in the old girl yet.

The realization he is speaking for something to say before he shuts his eyes and presses his foot harder, determined not to swerve.

The meat

The carcass hung in the shop for nine days till the edges congested and turned brown in the air.

People came and went. They bought wafers of beef, pale veal, ham from the slicer, joints, fillets, mutton chops. They took tomatoes and brown eggs, tins of fruit cocktail, cherries, handfuls of green parsley, bones. But no one wanted the meat. It dropped overhead from a claw hook, flayed and split down the spinal column: familiar enough in its way. It was cheap. But they asked for shin and oxtail, potted head, trotters. The meat refused to sell. Folk seemed embarrassed even to be caught keeking in its direction. One or two made tentative enquiries about a plate of sausages coiled to the left of the dangling shadow while the yellowing hulk hung restless, twisting on its spike. These were never followed through. The sausages sat on, pink and greasy, never shrinking by so much as a link. He moved the sausages to another part of the shop where they sold within the hour. Something about the meat was infecting.

By the tenth day, the fat on its surface turned leathery and translucent like the rind of an old cheese. Flies landed in the curves of the neck and he did not brush them away. The deep-set ball of bone sunk in the shoulder turned pale blue. There was no denying the fact: it had to be moved. The ribs were sticky and the smell had begun to repulse him, clogging the air in the already clammy interior of the shop, and he could detect its unmistakable seep under the door to his living room when he was alone in the evening. So he fetched a stool and reached out to the lard hook, seized the meat and with one accurate slice of the cleaver, cut it down. It languished on the sawdust floor till nightfall when he threw it into the back close parallel to the street. As he closed the shutter on the back door, he could hear the scuffling of small animals and strays.

In the morning, all that remained was the hair and a strip of tartan ribbon. These he salvaged and sealed in a plain wooden box beneath the marital bed. A wee minding.

Fearless

There would be days when you didn't see him and then days when you did. He just appeared suddenly, shouting threats up the main street, then went away again. You didn't question it. Nobody said anything to Fearless. You just averted your eyes when he was there and laughed about him when he wasn't. Behind his back. It was what you did.

Fearless was a very wee man in a greasy gaberdine coat meant for a much bigger specimen altogether. Grey-green sleeves dripped over permanent fists so just a row of yellow knuckles, like stained teeth, showed below the cuffs. One of these fisted hands carried a black, waxed canvas bag with an inept burst up one seam. He had a gammy leg as well, so every second step the bag clinked, a noise like a rusty tap, regular as a heartbeat. He wore a deceptively cheery bunnet like Paw Broon's over an escape of raw, red neck that hinted a crew cut underneath; but that would've meant he went to the barber's on a regular basis, keeping his hair so short, and sat in like everybody else waiting his turn, so it was hard to credit, and since you never saw him without the bunnet you never knew for sure. And he had these terrible specs. Thick as the bottoms of milk bottles, one lens patched with Elastoplast. Sometimes his eyes looked crossed through these terrible specs but it was hard to be sure because you didn't get to look long enough to see. Fearless wouldn't let you.

There was a general assumption he was a tramp. A lot of people called him a tramp because he always wore the same clothes and he was filthy but he wasn't a tramp. He had his own house down the shorefront scheme; big black finger stains round the keyhole and the curtains always shut. You could see him sometimes, scrabbling at the door to get in, looking suspiciously over his shoulder while he was forcing the key to fit. There were usually dirty plates on the doorstep too. The old woman next door cooked his meals and laid them on the step because he wouldn't answer the door. He sometimes took them and he sometimes didn't. Depended on his mood. Either way, there were usually dirty plates. The council cut his grass, he had daffodils for christsake—he wasn't a tramp. He was the kind that got tramps a bad name: dirty, foul-mouthed, violent, and drunk. He was an alkie all right, but not a tramp: the two don't necessarily follow.

The thing about Fearless was that he lived in a state of permanent anger. And the thing he was angriest about was being looked at. Sometimes he called it MAKING A FOOL OF and nobody was allowed to get away with it. It was a rule and he had to spend a lot of time making sure everybody knew it. He would storm up and down the main street, threatening, checking every face just in case they were look-ing then if he thought he'd caught you he would stop, stiffen and shout WHO ARE YOU TRYING TO MAKE A FOOL OF and attack. Sometimes he just attacked: depended on his mood. Your part was to work out what sort of mood it was and try and adjust to it, make the allowance. It was

what you were supposed to do. Most folk obliged, too—
went out of their way to avoid his maybe-squinty eyes or
pointedly NOT LOOK when they heard the clink and drag,
clink and drag, like Marley's ghost, coming up the street.
Then the air would fall ominously silent while he stopped,
checking out a suspicious back, reinforcing his law. On a
bad day, he would just attack anyway to be on the safe side.
Just in case. You couldn't afford to get too secure. There
was even a story about a mongrel stray he'd wound into a
half nelson because it didn't drop its gaze quick enough, but
that was probably just a story. Funnier than the catalog of
petty scraps, blows that sometimes connected and sometimes didn't that made up the truth. It might have been true
right enough but that wasn't the point. The point was you
were supposed to laugh. You were meant to think he was
funny. Fearless: the very name raised smiles and humorous
expectations. Women shouted their weans in at night with
HERE'S FEARLESS COMING, or squashed tantrums
with the warning YOU'LL END UP LIKE FEARLESS.
Weans made caricatures with hunchback shoulders, cross-
eyes and a limp. Like Richard the Third. A bogeyman. And
men? I have to be careful here. I belonged to the world of
women and children on two counts, so I never had access
to their private thoughts voiced in private places: the book-
ie's, the barber's, the pub. Maybe they said things in there
I can have no conception of. Some may have thought he
was a poor old soul who had gone to the bad after his wife
left him. Romantics. I suppose there were some who could
afford to be. Or maybe they saw him as an embarrassment,
a misfit, a joke. I don't know. What I do know is that I
never saw any of them shut him up when the anger started
or try and calm it down. I remember what women did:
leaving food on the doorstep and bottles for him to get
money on; I remember women shaking their heads as he
went past and keeping their eyes and their children low.

But I don't remember any men doing anything much at all. He didn't seem to touch their lives in the same way. They let him get on with what he did as his business. There was a kind of respect for what he was, almost as though he had a right to hurl his fists, spit, eff and blind—christ, some people seemed to admire this drunken wee tragedy as a local hero. They called him *a character. Fearless is a character right enough* they would say and smile, a smile that accounted for boys being boys or something like that. Even polismen did it. And women who wanted to be thought above the herd—one of the boys. After all, you had to remember his wife left him. It was our fault really. So we had to put up with it the way we put up with everything else that didn't make sense or wasn't fair; the hard, volatile maleness of the whole West Coast Legend. You felt it would have been shameful, disloyal even, to admit you hated and feared it. So you kept quiet and turned your eyes away.

It's hard to find the words for this even now. I certainly had none then, when I was wee and Fearless was still alive and rampaging. I would keek out at him from behind my mother's coat, watching him limp and clink up the main street and not understand. He made me sick with fear and anger. I didn't understand why he was let fill the street with himself and his swearing. I didn't understand why people ignored him. Till one day the back he chose to stop and stare at was my mother's.

We were standing facing a shop window, her hand in mine, thick through two layers of winter gloves. The shop window was full of fireplaces. And Fearless was coming up the street. I could see him from the other end of the street, closer and closer, clinking the black bag and wheeling at irregular intervals seeing if he could catch somebody looking. The shouting was getting louder while we stood, looking in at these fireplaces. It's unlikely she was actually interested in fireplaces: she was just doing what she was supposed to do in the hope he'd leave us alone—and teaching me to do the same. Fearless got closer. Then I saw his reflection in the glass: three days' growth, the bunnet, the taped-up specs. He had jerked round, right behind where we were standing and stopped. He looked at our backs for a long time, face contorted with indecision. What on earth did he think we were plotting, a woman and a wean in a pixie hat? What was it that threatened? But something did and he stared and stared, making us bide his time. I was hot and cold at once, suddenly sick because I knew it was our turn, our day for Fearless. I closed my eyes. And it started. A lot of loud, jaggy words came out the black hole of his mouth. I didn't know the meanings but I felt their pressure. I knew they were bad. And I knew they were aimed at my mother. I turned slowly and looked: a reflex of outrage beyond my control. I was staring at him with my face blazing and I couldn't stop. Then I saw he was staring back with these pebble-glass eyes. The words had stopped. And I realized I was looking at Fearless.

There was a long second of panic, then something else did the thinking for me. All I saw was a flash of white sock with my foot attached, swinging out and battering into his shin. It must have hurt me more than it hurt him but I'm not all that clear on the details. The whole thing did not finish as heroically as I'd have liked. I remember Fearless limping away, clutching the ankle with his free hand and shouting about a liberty, and my mother shaking the living daylights out of me, a furious telling off, and a warning I'd be found dead strangled up a close one day and never to do anything like that again.

It was all a long time ago. My mother is dead, and so, surely, is Fearless. But I still hear something like him; the chink and drag from the close-mouth in the dark, coming across open, derelict spaces at night, blustering at bus stops where I have to wait alone. With every other woman, though we're still slow to admit it, I hear it, still trying to lay down the rules. It's more insistent now because we're less ready to comply, look away and know our place. And I still see men smiling and ignoring it because they don't give a damn. They don't need to. It's not their battle. But it was ours and it still is. I hear my mother too and the warning is never far away. But I never could take a telling.

The outrage is still strong, and I kick like a mule.

Scenes from the
Life No. 27:
Living In

*A spacious room. One side is dominated by a wall-shelving unit
with a stereo, video, recording units, speakers and amps, some
books and a* huge *TV. There are also some bottles and cans of
lager as a "cocktail" section. A modern armchair sits squarely in
front of this unit, facing the glowing green lights of the sound
system. A few open books on the carpet, an overturned (empty)
wineglass, a Rubik's Cube or some such "adult" toy. Opposite
these, a desk, a drawing board. Lots of crumpled paper and writing
things on the desk. There is a large mirror and a corkboard above
it. Some plants.*

*Between, deeper into the room, a sleeping area with a large bed,
wardrobe with set-in mirror, bedside table and a canvas chair. On
the bed, a thick disheveled duvet. The fitted carpet is strewn with
cast-off clothes, a pair of trousers hang over the chair arm.*

*Furnishings throughout are tasteful but pedestrian: everything self-
colored in subdued shades. Nothing is patterned; none of the plants
are flowering or exotic. No cushions; no ornaments on the shelves.*

*To one side, in a corner, is a sectioned-off bathroom with a per-
manently opened door: it should not seem too separate from the*

rest of the room. The sink and toilet bowl are clearly visible. There are lots of jars, bottles and tubes ranged along the back of the sink and on shelves. Behind the sink, an enormous mirror. The toilet seat is up. There is a towel crumpled on the floor, and another draped untidily over the bath rim.

Light enters from a sloping skylight above the bed, angled to make visible a diamond of greyish sky. Light level should suggest an extremely overcast day, twilight—something of that sort. The same level obtains for almost the entire play.

Articles on the floor interjoin the different areas of the room.
There is also a telephone, coffee table, poster on one wall.
There is no kitchen apparent.
Other minor properties will be indicated in the text.

Note for the actor.
TONY *is entirely suggested through improvised movement.* Never speak. TONY *is at all times a presentable and pleasing figure, trim and tall (though not excessively so), fashionably good-looking. His clothes and hairstyle are neat and businesslike, but he wears them with a casual stylishness (or vice versa). Maintain his neat appearance by occasionally checking that cuffs, trouser crease, etc. are as they should be, smooth down hair, check shoulders . . . but keep this unobtrusive.* TONY's *movements are graceful and masculine: even at his most relaxed he has dignity. He is smooth and unhurried, never coarse or clumsy. His movements and any noise he makes (humming or sighing, spitting out water, etc.) are restrained, almost self-conscious.*
Never alter his expression. *The steady but eager blankness of* TONY's *face throughout is essential to a correct interpretation of the character. Never slip from character or acknowledge the audience in any way.*

Act 1

Half-light. A fairly lengthy stasis before a digital watch alarm begins to play "Clementine" thinly. The lumpy duvet twitches and moves. Slowly, the head and hands of a man appear from the top. It is TONY: his eyes still closed. The watch continues to sing through his waking ritual. His feet find the carpet first, then his torso rises to let him sit with his head hanging forward over his knees, the corner of the duvet still hiding his crotch. He reaches for the watch, silences the music, straps it to his wrist. In slow stages, he rises, stretching a muscular body. He has been wearing blue cotton briefs in bed. Only now does he open his eyes. (He does not contort his face to wakefulness—even newly emerged from sleep, he is a handsome man.) He blinks a good deal on the way to the bathroom where he picks up the fallen towel at his feet and drops it over the edge of the bath before standing poised at the toilet bowl. With his back to the audience, he empties his bladder, soundlessly, and without undue disturbance to the blue briefs. Now he takes a few squares of white toilet paper to carefully wrap his penis and nestle it gently back inside the briefs. (Allow time and precision for these maneuvers, which are to be executed with utmost discretion; it should not be possible for even the most prudish member of the audience to take offense here.)

Once this routine is accomplished, he carries on with the rest of his preparations: running the taps at full power to wash his face and drying it vigorously with the towel, sponging under his arms and across his chest then brushing his teeth thoroughly. (NB: a bearded actor will be able to take much longer over this part by spending time trimming the beard and mustache into the sink.) Once he has finished, the damp towel is once more relegated to the floor. TONY turns his attentions to the lotions and unguents on the shelves: he carries this out routinely. First, he applies roll-on deodorant to his armpits, then sprinkles some talc on his chest, rubbing it into the skin with firm, long strokes. Next, he selects a bottle of after-shave to dash some into his hands and slap into his face and neck (neck only if bearded). He may also add a discreet touch to his pubic hair as an afterthought—gingerly. He examines his face for some time in the large bathroom mirror, flicking away a fallen eyelash, checking a dubious patch of skin, inspecting his teeth, etc. *The expression of his face never alters.* After this, he turns back to the bottles and tubes, sprays something under his arms from an aerosol, adds a touch more after-shave, brushes his teeth again, and strokes his neck.

Fully awake now, he moves purposefully and decisively back into the main part of the room and begins an assault on dressing. He begins with the trousers over the edge of the canvas chair, putting them on as he stands, then adds the items strewn on the floor in turn: a white shirt, a dark tie, pair of dark socks. Last are the dark shoes at the side of the bed. Checks himself over in the wardrobe mirror: he looks *good*. Now he rakes his hair with his fingers, combs it through into place (replacing the comb in his trouser pocket) and shakes his head to naturalize the effect to his satisfaction. A jacket from the wardrobe completes the out-fit: he drapes it cavalierly over one shoulder. Expression-lessly triumphant, he gazes at his neat reflection (he does not smile).

Eyes still on his mirror self, he checks for wallet, keys and cash by patting at various appropriate pockets. He is ready. Erect, he marches out and off through the audience. He looks fine, assured, masculine. Fathomless.

Act 2

The room as it was left. Nothing is different. Street noise begins to filter through the skylight, making the room seem all the more still and quiet within. Then a series of distinct and discrete sounds, building in volume so the last in the series is very loud indeed.

1. General traffic noise, cars ticking over, etc.
2. A motorbike running, then revving repeatedly.
3. A car taking a corner too fast.
4. Drunken singing and cursing, indistinct obscenities.
5. A clicking of shoes on a pavement, then jeering: the banter of men catcalling. It becomes progressively more blatant and aggressive then stops. A burst of wolf whistling.
6. Chanting (football slogans?) and a breaking bottle.
7. Some grunting and scuffling; the sound of running and angry obscenities.
8. Silence. An earsplitting wolf whistle.

The diamond of sky in the skylight glows and changes to a very bright blue then dims to its usual wash.

Act 3

TONY walks through the audience and back onstage. His jacket slewed over his shoulder and his collar loosened suggest a hard day. He throws down the car keys onto the coffee table and drops the jacket on the floor before turning on the radio. It plays soft music interspersed with long sentences—not particularly audible. He selects a can from the shelves then sits to peel it open and spread comfortably in the chair, the can in one hand, sipping every so often with his eyes closed. The radio plays and he eases into relaxation. The man, the can and the radio make a soothing triangle for at least ten minutes. Then he opens his eyes to press the button that activates the *huge* TV. He sits up to look into the screen briefly and finish the remains of the can. It shows discontinuous bits of old films—Westerns, adventure stories, gangster movies, etc.—bits of detective serials, car chases and adverts, sometimes cartoon figures and newsreel. The volume is very low. Rising, TONY begins to wander about the room, picking up the odd book, riffling through his record collection, etc. Soon, he takes another can with a long glance at the part-nude figure on the back before tearing off the ring-pull. He drinks from this through his tour, making inspections, mental digressions. He is at peace, relaxed in his ownership of the place: he is a man in his own home. At some stage, he may put a record on the stereo; again very softly. The combined volume of the radio, TV and disk are never too obtrusive or harsh. Eventually, he looks at his watch and settles into the easy chair, selecting his favored channel. It shows the same as the other one. He falls asleep facing the TV and the green indicator lights of the stereo deck. By turns, the noises of the machines fall away, till there is only a soft crackle sifting from the TV. It is then that TONY wakes, dropping the empty can on the carpet. He looks round, rises, rubbing his neck, and goes to the bathroom.

His evening ablutions are much less mannered and shorter than those of the morning: he washes and dries his face and brushes his teeth. Even the water runs less forcefully. He slackens his trousers and pees noisily into the toilet bowl, shakes his penis and discards the tissue from his briefs into the bowl before flushing. His flies undone, he comes through to sit on the bed where he undresses. Trousers return to the canvas chair; the shoes and socks, shirt and tie lie where they are dropped. Without rising, he swings his legs up to slot under the still-disheveled duvet, removes and sets his watch, then places it on the bedside table. He has finished with the day: he sinks well under the warmth of the duvet and rolls away from the audience to sleep.

Everything is still for a long time.

Next to the recumbent figure, the lumps in the duvet move. Minutely at first, then more noticeably they move toward TONY then undulate in small rhythmic patterns above his body. TONY inhales loudly: the movements stop: he rolls abruptly away, back out to the audience. There is silence and stillness and TONY's eyes shut very tightly. Nothing happens for a few minutes. Another mild movement behind him. He sighs deeply, sets his mouth hard and rolls onto his face. Another period of immobility and stillness. TONY's form relaxes slowly, completely. He has fallen asleep.

Stars appear in the strip of sky above the bed. They glow very brightly as the set darkens till the shape of TONY in the bed has a silver outline. The bed pulses again: there is something under the lumps in the duvet—something *is* the lumps in the duvet. It moves again, then emerges in one sweep to stand at the end of the bed. It is a naked woman. Soundlessly she moves round to look down at the sleeping man, stroking the place above his head with one hand, taking great care not to touch. Then she moves more centrally to face the enormous mirror at the wardrobe. She stares and stands steadfastly, unblinking so her eyeballs shine in the dark; and through the gloom her skin looks very pale and downy, starlit. Gently, liquidly, with spread fingers, she traces her hands lightly over her body: lingering on her shoulders, over each breast caressingly in turn, stroking across her ribs and down, over her stomach, firmly and repeatedly across her thighs and hips: soothing strokes. This takes some time and cannot be rushed if the right effect is to be achieved. Her deep concentration, intensity and absorption in the task, the feel of skin under the fingertips are paramount. Then, nearing completion, one hand glides upward to clasp a shoulder and shield her breasts as the fingers of the other fan deep into her pubic hair. Head erect, she looks into the mirror, into the white contours of her body curving out of the darkness.

TONY sleeps.

Addendum

Note for the actress.
Extreme stillness is demanded for the part. No one is to know she is there until the moment comes. The audience must never be sure whether she is substantial or not.

Nightdriving

I.

and he was missing the kids and couldn't sleep so we drove
down to the shore, right past the barriers and warning signs
to the edge of the cob, the headlights swinging out across
the drop to the sand. It was so dark I couldn't see anything
over the water from the other side and the sea was just a
noise like nervous cellophane, like cellophane crushing in
someone's hands. He got out, walking with his back melting
in the dark till he was just a blur at the end of the breakwater,
a milky stain coming and going in the pitch-black middle
of the noise of the sea and the wind outside. And I sat on
in the car, twisting to see past where the headlamps cut a
wedge across the sand. The rushes showed white needles in
the dips of the dunes; dunes and flakes of litter in the ash-
color sand. And I was frightened. I opened the door shouting
I'M COMING TOO, I'M COMING WITH YOU but the
wind blotted up in my mouth and I knew there would be
no answer. There would be no answer because I couldn't
be heard. Then I started to walk to the edge of the cob,
stumbling over shale, afraid I'd fall and tear my hands on

the edges of broken shells. So I stopped. I stopped because there was no help for it and stood peering out at the visible sand, searching for what I couldn't see. It was too dark. Yet I didn't want to show how scared I was, keeping looking for movements through the dunes in case anyone was there, in case something was coming. Only a crazy person would be out there in the middle of the night in this howling wind but I kept looking out, into the hard echo of the waves I couldn't see, over the strip of grey sand thinking *There is something more I can't make sense of, something more to come* and getting colder and colder. He was still out there at the end of the breakwater and there was still no answer. The rushes on the dunes were rippling like hair, the battered ends of the waves falling beaten on the shore. The waves kept coming inshore.

2.

since visiting was very free but I was never sure if he would come. The floor was soft so it was sometimes sudden when he did appear, walking silently down the tunnel of striplight: his steady walk to where he knew I would wait. And we went out across the soft tiles to the fresh night air and the borders of the car park outside, slipping our hips between the cold metal curves of people's motors. He strapped the seat belt tight across my chest to hold me down then he'd cough the ignition and the tires cracked over gravel toward the motorway and we'd go speeding down the motorway in pure white lines. He would press the accelerator hard so I sank back into the leather, the seat belt gripping my chest and clothes spreading black against the green leather skins. He would wear blue. Then we'd snake out onto the open lanes and uphill, the whole frame lifting while he reached to turn the music loud with one hand on the wheel. And the rising and the music would fill up inside the car; pressing my spine, bowling me back against the falling leather so I could hardly bear it. Sometimes he would smile from the corner of his mouth, feeling for overdrive with one hand on the wheel and we were tearing down the white lanes, their patterns in the mirror streaming behind like ribbons on the wind. And all I could see on my back were the overcrowding stars of the streetlights, the yellow v-strip dazzling through the music swelling up like bursting glass on the curved road back to the ward.

3.

It's not my car but someone lets me use it if I promise to be careful coming home late. The road I have to travel is treacherous and twists through countryside so there are no lights to mark the edges, just the solid dark that rises with the hills on either side. There are never many cars. You see headlamps float over dips in the darkness and know there must be a road beneath: an unseen path below the rise and fall of the beams in the blackness on either side. And sometimes you see nothing. Not until they slew from nowhere, too close from a corner that didn't exist before, a hidden side road or farmhouse track. Light veers under your fingernails and there is a second of sudden wakefulness, too much brightness in the car from the other presence outside. You see your own grey hands wrapping the wheel, the swirl of grass like water in the gutters. Then somehow it's over. Only the red smears of taillights dwindling in the mirror show it was ever there and you are driving on. The steering leather under your fists, its turning. The road looks new. It looks like nowhere you have been before.

And you remember.
You keep driving and remember.

The city road is a narrow stretch with hills that rise on either side, steep like the sides of a coffin: a lining of grass like green silk and the lid open to the sky but it is a coffin all the same. The verges hang with ripped-back cars from the breaker's yard, splitting the earth on either side, but you keep on going, over the dips and bends between the rust and heather till the last blind bend and it appears. Between the green and brown, the husks of broken cars: a v-shaped glimpse of somewhere else so far away it seems to float. It's distant and beautiful and no part of the rest: no part of the road I am traveling through, not Ayrshire, not Glasgow. It comes and goes behind a screen as I drive toward it, a piece of city waiting in the v-shaped sky if this is my day to make a split-second mistake. It's always there. And I know too it's simply the way home. I accelerate because it is not today. I am still here.
Driving.

things he said

Awkward, the two of us virtual strangers going to a concert and shy. I wanted to know what he thought of the music, friend of a friend, someone who looked as though he was on the verge of saying something all the time.

London is lonely he said; easy enough on the phone, the things he said in those odd inflections, just the voice and that detached, since I hardly knew the set of his face. That closeness, a scandalous thing between virtual strangers, letting the unfamiliar voice coil into an ear but allowable so it didn't feel out of place offering: he could stay over, his going to London the next morning and the train easier from where I lived. The mouthpiece breathing after he said yes and I thought we could talk.

The concert was something agreed, neither of us able to look the other in the eye yet, a place to be that was not personal. The things he said were particular. We thought the same things about the music and that made it better, made us relax. It was raining when we went out, running to be clear of it. The two grey flight bags, one with a bottle bulky in the pocket, made red marks on his hands.

Going up the stairs, neither of us spoke. He left the bags in the hall, fished out the wine. On separate seats, awkward, the two of us virtual strangers alone in the same room for the first time but determined, we tried to feel at home. The things he said. That kisses were a threat, not able to be direct. Sexuality became a byword, leaning forward on the chair and flexing his hands, my fingers on the neck of a glass. Kisses were a threat, a resonance at the back of his throat before he looked me in the eye. If you get the men and women thing right, everything else follows. The angle of his arm, his eyes huge. I said maybe you'd like to lie down now but there was something else to drink, something else to drink. Finding more to say, lighting cigarettes and holding the bottle by the neck, never letting his eyes shift. The things he said, not ready himself for how much. And when he stopped, knowing I was there, that the things he said put me past sleep, he stood up. Smoke trailing over his lip like gauze, the rims of his eyes grey.

Cold in the kitchen at five-thirty, his arms opened without thought.

The things he did.

A Week with Uncle Felix

"Clementine."
The buzzing came clearer by degrees.

Duncan humming through the engine noise, the same bit over and over. Grace was muttering at the same time, paper crackling under her thumbs. She could hear clearly now, head pressed into the car window, that comforting rattle of the skull that made you want to hold on to the moments of being not awake. Not yet. The shuffle and the cough: you could feel her turning, drawing breath.

Here. Sleepy.

Grace's voice closer than she'd expected. Then a bump and grind of gravel shuddering up through the tires as the car tilted under some ragged shade. The engine shudder bounced the damp glass under her cheek then cut to nothing.

Here, Teeny. Teeny Leek.

Grace knew fine she would only be pretending now, but she wasn't bothering, just zipping up the bag ready to get out.

Rise and shine.

The front doors opened and shut again, leaving her to it.

The girl opened her eyes. Squeals starting up already. Cards slithered on the blanket as she turned to see. People were outside, through that fog on the window, merging and separating on the silent grey grass. Duncan looked even shorter when he stood next to her like that. Like Olive Oyl and Popeye and smiling too much. The other one was even taller than Grace. There was a movement like dancing before they fuzzed over completely. Lifting the sleeve made more cards fall. She was reaching for them when something moved outside, rustling the branches, veering close to the glass. Then the catch clicked, a swirl of night air retracting her legs under the tartan. Leopard skin with shadow, the man crouched in the open doorframe. Uncle Felix.

Out you come Sweetheart.
One shiny eye free of the patches of dark. It took a moment to realize who the Sweetheart was. Then whether it was a joke. He was holding out his hand.
Out you come.

Things spilling as she inched forward, unpeeling her thighs from the vinyl, crumpled sweetie papers rolling at her feet like colored beads. Making a mess as usual. She was stooping to pick them up when the hand fell on her shoulder. It wrapped the whole bone.
Never mind that, love. It'll keep.
His eyes were the color of old paper.
You don't remember.
The English accent, the lips disappearing when he smiled.
Long time ago, love. Uncle Felix, your dad's brother. Hello pet.
Grace's face pushed into the space between them, creasy and moon-colored in the dark.
Just like your daddy, that's what we always say isn't it right? Just like our Jock. Do you remember Uncle eh? She likely won't remember.

Her teeth slipped and she bit down to make them lock back.

Let's away into the warm. We can do all this in the house eh?

Duncan clicked his tongue. It meant he was hungry.

I'll do this and youse get on in.

He threw the keys up and bounced them off his shoe into his hand: a party trick to make them laugh. They all did. The man moved first, turning on his heel and roping an arm round his sister.

I get the best bit as usual.

They had the same kind of mouth. Duncan was already picking things up, grunting to get by his stomach.

That's right enough. Like as two peas. Two peeolas.

Grace's voice fading, red gravel frying under her shoes.

The path was outlined in light from the door, dented net curtain in the window: he would have been looking out to see if they were coming. A smell of night stock got heavier as she walked. No roses though. Her mother had said there would be roses. The man went on inside while Grace stayed behind on the porch, making a performance of wiping her shoes. They didn't need it but it was manners, it was what you did. The girl stopped and did the same, looking in past the door. Black beams lined the hall ceiling till they disappeared through the wall at the far end. Beams for heaven's sake. Scrolls on the green hall carpet. And these horrible school slip-ons. Grace was watching her, that smile she did when she thought you didn't know she was doing it, lumpy veins right down to the backs of the flat shoes. They'd stopped marching now.

Age before beauty eh? That right?

The woman went first.

Felix was in the kitchen, finishing at the gas and sitting the kettle on the bloom of flames. Through the acrid match smell, she caught a thickness of sauce and spice: man smells. Grace didn't seem to notice. She was into a cupboard and rummaging for something without being asked. The girl sat on a corner of cold marble table as the man swirled water from a rubber-nosed tap into a brown teapot then turned to look at her, folding his arms and leaning back against the sink.

Quiet one, aren't you? What are you thinking pet?

With nothing to say, the girl smiled and looked at her feet. The toes were scuffed as well. Grace rattled about with tea stuff, oblivious. It would have been good if she'd said something but then Grace didn't always hear what folk were saying. The man kept staring. Sooner or later he would say something about looking like her father. That was usually what folk said, sometimes with the jings crivvens stuff about her age: Only eleven, they grow up that quick these days and so on. People always said something and it was usually just for something to say. She could feel the stare from here. It would have been good to go over to the window and look out, pretend to be interested but there was nothing to see, just bits of kitchen reflecting on the black. She yawned. The man thought it was funny.

Straight to bed, I should think. You've had a long day.

Eight hours on the road and she's been good as gold. Grace flourished the teapot. She was putting on that cute voice she did, like a cartoon mouse.

Can amuse herself that one, no trouble to anybody. Am I right?

That's what I remember, he said. Never a cheep out of you last time either.

Don't remember, do you? said Grace. She doesn't, eh? She doesn't remember.

The voice was starting to get on her nerves. It was embarrassing and it was also wrong because she did remember. She remembered lying in the big room listening and the door opening, the big shape of a man coming in from the outside to pick her up, the cold off the buttons on his coat. The smell of tobacco. He had carried her, just carried her about till she went back to sleep or something. Another time, somebody that was probably her mother repeating the same words: Say thank you, say thank you for the nice present. And she had run away. She couldn't remember what the present was but she remembered him being there all right. Remembering hadn't anything to do with it though. She wasn't really being asked at all.

You don't remember, eh? Dozy? Dozy Dora?

Grace was just showing off. The girl looked back at the floor and Felix laughed.

Right then! I'll take you up. It's all ready: changed sheets, the lot. Waiting since yesterday.

The hand held out to show the way to the hall.

Ladies first.

There was a row of photographs up the stair wall, shiny behind frames. He stopped halfway up, pointing one out; black-and-white going brown. It had twelve blurry young men in matching outfits and hats, all laughing and waving at the camera. His nail tapped at one of the uniforms in the back row.

Me. RAF Bisley 1944. Good looking eh?

She smiled a bit and peered to please him but it didn't look like anybody, just an arrangement of grey under a hat brim.

Good times with the bad, love.

The top stairs creaked and there was more of the green carpet on the landing. He showed her three doors that were the bedrooms and bathroom, then another piece of staircase past the window where you could hardly see it. He put on a switch, lighting up the door at the top in fits and starts. The bulb was faulty.

And up here, all yours.

His back flashed off and on as they walked.

Upstairs, the room was stuffy with stale sunlight as though the window had been closed a long time. He was already pulling curtains when she went in, hanging the black space with flowers and leaves. There were rosebuds on the quilt, matching stuff. Single bed; they shared the double at home.

This all right, madam? He rubbed dust off the bedside shade. Nobody uses it much these days.

The last word stamped out by feet, thumping up from the landing.

Lovely, she said, but he couldn't hear her right. She was shouting it again as Duncan breenged in out of breath, pushing past to drop the case on the mattress. The whole bed shook.

Straight to bed she says. Up the stairs she says.

He mopped his brow, pretending the case was heavy, and looked at the other man.

Just this minute here and tired already eh?

They smiled at each other: a tall thin man and a wee fat man sharing her from opposite ends of the rug. They were all looking at the case. It was burst up one side. They kept old sheets in it at home, stuffed at the back of a cupboard.

Well then.

More looks and nods.

Goodnight love.

The words hung on in the space as the door closed; fainter creaking on the stairs, muttering and laughter. The case was still rocking on the bedsprings.

Morning showed a wicker chair, dresser, bookcase with no books. Wallpaper with roses. She could see without having to open the curtains. And no need to lie dead still for ages;

nobody to moan you'd been kicking in your sleep or you'd taken all the blankets. She stretched to use up all the space deliberately. Her mother could be doing the same thing, this same minute. On you go, take her. Do me good to get rid of her for a week. Sometimes she laughed when she said things like that and sometimes not. This time not. Grace said Och Greta then pretended she thought it was a joke. But it didn't matter now. It was good to be here: your own bed, your own room. First thing in the morning, whole holiday to go and England outside. You could do anything you liked.

Up and rummaging through the case, she remembered. There would be problems with the bathroom downstairs. The bathroom downstairs and there being men about the place. She couldn't go down the way she would have at home, straight out of bed in the white knickers and bra. They'd see you. Not just men: Uncle Felix. He used to be in the RAF for heaven's sake, the photo they had of him in the chocolate box where he looked like Clark Gable with the wee mustache and Brylcreem. They had lots of that photo: her mother liked it. The Best of a Bad Shower. Not like the other four he'd come off with their po-faces and dirty nails. Not like Your Bloody Father. Fancy manners and the English accent, even his name something different. You didn't walk around in front of a man like that in day-old underwear, things you had slept in. Dressing gowns made sense after all. Proper people had dressing gowns. There wasn't anything like one either. It would have to be the fresh T-shirt and yesterday's jeans. And being quick. She'd have to be quick.

Grace was there at the foot of the landing, looking pink.
    There you are. Your uncle Felix isn't in there.
She meant the bathroom.

On you go and hurry up, then we can go down together.
I'll wait.

She stood right outside, shouting at the door. It got fainter
when the girl turned on the tap, like a chicken up a tunnel:
harmless but not quite human. But it didn't go away. Her
own name too many times: Senga. Senga, Senga, Senga.
She ran the tap harder and sank her face into the water.

The smell of fish and coffee came halfway up the stairs. The
kitchen was misty with it. Felix stood with his back to the
sink, eating the substance of the fish smell from a blue
plate.

Well, Grace said, rolling her eyes. Well.

There were four poached eggs in a soup plate in the middle
of the table beside a box of unidentifiable cereal, toast, butter, and different jars. Grace stood for a minute looking.
They were being spoilt she said. She couldn't think, just
could not and she'd never recover from the spoiling. There
wasn't anything to serve with so she had to get up again as
soon as she sat down. There weren't any bowls either. The
girl took toast. Felix smiled through hairy bones, dislodging
something from between his back teeth.

How about town this morning? Plans in the offing?

Grace served herself an egg. He stretched and walked across
to the girl's chair.

Shops, miniature village maybe.

The chair dipped as he leaned his weight against it, rumbling
the last word along the spars into her back. There was a
faint tang of fish from his breath.

I'm going that way anyway. Take you in if you like.

You'll like that.

Grace chewed a piece of crust, drizzling milk into the girl's
tea.

Likes history you know. History and all that kind of
thing. Good at the school.

Black bits on the sides of her mouth and her teeth were silted.

No need to rush: take your time, ladies, take your time. We've all day. All week if we want. The chair creaked as he released his grip and walked to the window. All week. He lit a cigarette with the match inside his hand, first draw.

Trying not to walk on the cracks. The wee boy tottered, his hand reaching for the steeple. He deliberately didn't grab at the last minute and fell, the hand thumping into the cemetery wall before his mother came and picked him up, howling. They stood back from the model church to let them past, the boy with blood on his knees, to the toilet on the other side of the entrance queue. Grace had got a fright but at least he hadn't knocked anything over.

Need to be more careful. Specially when it's busy.
It was worse than busy but they stuck to the path with the other tourists, squeezing by the edges of the miniature houses to see the details. It was what they'd come to do. Window displays in the tiny shops, real flowers in the park and the graveyard. It was probably better than the real thing because they'd missed out the public toilets and the housing scheme, things like that. Grace said you had to admit it was nice. She admitted it herself umpteen times. If you looked closely though you could see staples holding the thatch onto the real thatched cottage but it didn't seem right to say. You probably weren't meant to look that close and it would just be twisted. It would put Grace in the huff as well. Anyway, it *was* nice. Nice enough. Felix hadn't come: just let them out at the corner then drove off somewhere else, leaving the two of them on their own. There was no real reason to be annoyed by it. She was probably just too hot. They did another lap then bought tea and hot dogs from a van just

inside the park gate. Grace paid, handing over the paper cup and screwing her eyes up because of the sun. They were having a good time to themselves, just the two of them. Maybe they'd try the shops next. All the bins at the exit were full. They left their cups rolling at the side of the wire mesh, dribbling the dregs of tea.

Postcards were easy: nearly everywhere sold them. Other things took longer. There wasn't a supermarket: four antique shops, a cheese shop and an Edinburgh Woollen Mill but no supermarket. They only needed messages for the week. A couple of streets away, they found stalls and single shops that would do. A butcher in a daft straw hat wasn't pleased about the Scots fiver and snapped it open toward the light, peering while Grace said she was sorry. He took it eventually when she said there wasn't anything else and said how bonnie he thought the wee Scots lassies were to show there were no hard feelings. They didn't buy anything else till they went to the bank. They walked back and found a note behind the taps to say Duncan and Felix wouldn't be back till teatime.

Well that's fine, she said. Gets them out the road. We'll can do what we like as well then.

She lifted a lump wrapped in tracing paper. It started changing color while she held it up in her hand. They'd have a cup of something and a rest. A rest more than anything else. A nice rest. Then she saw the blood oozing down her arm in a twisted line and shouted. The meat was dripping on the lino as well. Senga went upstairs without waiting for the tea.

The attic was quiet, curtains were still closed from the morning, the bed still unmade. She'd forgotten about that. She didn't make beds often; even when she made the effort they weren't done right anyway. The case was open at the side, things jumbled on the top. They would crease. Only here a day and all this to tidy up. Not yet though, not now. Maybe Grace was right: a wee rest would be good. She was maybe still tired from yesterday; traveling made you tired. Grace would probably go for a lie down as well. She sat on the edge of the fankled sheets and tilted back onto the pillows. Then she saw the photograph: a plain frame behind the lamp on the bedside, obvious enough though she hadn't seen it last night. It was the one of her waiting in front of a brick wall in a white net dirndl skirt, staring up at the sun under that daft hat. A handbag as well. Sunday School Trip. When you looked hard something about the eyes was the same but not much. It wasn't really her at all, just a six-year-old wean waiting for a bus. There was something written along the bottom. *Senga, Jock's girl, Saltcoats.* Neat handwriting like a woman's. There was another photo as well, flat and dusty on the bottom of the cabinet shelf: pale cream and brown profile of her father now she brought it out to see. He never smiled in photos. Dour, her mother said. Twisted. It was the same mouth that Grace had, Felix as well. She looked back at the picture of herself. She wasn't smiling either. Both pictures slotted back into the same dust marks before she pulled the covers over her head for shade.

A face inflated over the rim of sheets when she opened her eyes. It was Duncan, smirking. Everybody was wondering where she had got to, he said, eyes huge behind the specs. A terrible lassie. Always tired. Ha ha. He ran his hand over the top of her head and said to be quick.

The tea wasn't ready at all. There was just a clutter of cutlery on the table and place mats. Offering to set places would never have occurred: they ate off their knees at home, in front of the TV. But there was this table here, a bit of the house for eating and nothing else in the corner of the living room. The men were watching TV somewhere else. She could hear the news reading itself as she struggled with lefts and rights, forks and spoons. It was good: the men at their business while she set the table. It was what you did, what proper people did off the leash of know-nothing, couthy Ayrshire and a house with no men. That thing with the salt and pepper shakers would be a mustard pot, a spoon sticking out the side. Like yellow oil paint. Even the smell.

Cooee.

Grace's face poked through a hole in the wall. Then her hands pushing out plates and disappearing again when the girl took them, back to the noise of pots. The men appeared, knowing without being told and started pulling out chairs, talking loud about football then Grace came through with the other plates, smaller ones. Senga gave her two to the men. Duncan said he was starving. He always said it. Felix cleared his throat.

Ladies and gentleman, tonight we do things in style.

He brought a bottle out from under the table. Grace squawked and clapped.

Only one though—don't want to overdo it.

The glasses were out along the bureau. Grace and Duncan exchanged a look as he poured four and Senga tried to look as though she knew she was being spoiled and appreciated it. They held the glasses out into the middle of the table when Felix did it.

Blood ties, he said. To us.

They clinked raggedly, all smiles. It tasted like thick metal in the mouth, the smell of warm pennies. Grace said Well! and pretended to be dizzy as he poured her some more. She was in a better mood and everything was going to be fine. At the other side of the table, Duncan sunk his knife into the chicken breast and asked for salt.

. . .

White.

The curtains split in one tug to leave her standing like a crucifix inside the drench of light. Just brightness at first. Then isolated islands of green as she uncreased her eyes, joining to a lawn and two rows of trees, eight or so, close enough for their branches to meet over the channel of grass. An elbow of branch was leaning on the sill outside, spreading leaves against the window. And something else now she looked, flat, purple smears like lipstick mouths. She moved her hand to see better. Plums. Attached to the ends of thin sticks where they were growing. Living things. There were more in the garden, dark shapes among the green when you looked. Beyond that, the high fencing where the wall of sky attached and went straight up without stopping. A string of pale butterflies knotted to the fencing with green thread. Sweet peas. There were no hills behind the tops of the trees and no sea in the distance. Second day here and this was the first she'd seen the view. First she'd opened the curtains, that's why. Lazy bitch. Imagining her mother saying it made her laugh out loud. Plums right outside for heaven's sake. She rapped the glass with her knuckles and watched them shiver.

Downstairs, Grace was at the sink, pasty in a print dress and open sandals, bare toes poking out.

Hello, stranger.

She went on rinsing cups and didn't turn round. The coffee smell meant that Felix had been and gone: it wouldn't have been made for anybody else. Grace stood to one side to let her by with the kettle.

You could make some for Uncle Duncan, she said. He's out with the motor.

She had on her headache face, rinsing the same cup for ages.

Never done with his motor.

The girl put tea straight into the mugs. Never mind about the bits. Safer than rooting about near the sink for the pot. It would also be good to get out. You couldn't ask what was the matter because she'd make out it was nothing and maybe take the huff because you'd suggested it. Worse, she would make out she hadn't taken the huff either. At least the milk and stuff was out on the table so there was no need to ask for anything and risk it. The teaspoon as well. Duncan took six sugars. She managed to stir them in silently. The spoon didn't even whisper.

Aye aye.

Duncan levered slowly out from under the bonnet, sighing. Cheers, he said. The mug had a grease stripe already: his hands were black. For a moment she wondered if she should ask if Grace was all right then knew she wouldn't. He likely wouldn't say either. Some things he just blanked out. Like the time they hit a dog coming back along the Dalry road at night in the car. He got out a minute, came back in, turned the ignition and just kept driving with his eyes set on the road. She'd been just about hysterical but knew not to speak. The one time she got near it, he started whistling. He drove her straight home and said what a nice run they'd had. A nice run. Neither of them had ever mentioned it again. He looked at her over the white rim, closing his throat.

How's the girl the day then?

Fine, she said.

Questions like that weren't really questions at all. It was embarrassing. Neither said anything for a while. Duncan took another mouthful of tea.

Nice place eh? Front green and everything.

I saw the garden out the back this morning, she said. Sweet peas. You can see them from the window.

You know who was the sweet pea man? Your dad liked the sweet peas. He was the boy for the flowers all right. Green fingers.

He blinked and shook his head.

Sweet peas and roses: that was your daddy. That was Jock all right.

There were no flowers at home, unless you counted the poppies that came up between the potatoes. They had potatoes and rhubarb, occasionally cabbage. Things you could eat. Duncan belched and sighed.

Your aunty June's garden that one.

He was wanting to tell a story.

Never met June, sure you didn't.

The story was OK. There was a long bit about the RAF and planting things, getting the garden nice for Felix retiring. Then when it happened it wasn't like anybody expected. He was out of the RAF only four weeks. June was pruning currant bushes and got tired, went for a lie down. Duncan looked into the bottom of the mug, tapped his nail on the rim. The Scottish side weren't asked to the funeral, of course. Too far away and too little notice. Still you'd have liked to have been asked. She waited for a moment then realized it was finished and didn't know what to say. It was like when he sang those terrible songs about Lonesome Cowboys or Old Shep; he liked you to look sad when he sang them. Grace did it as well. The worst was the time they went to the sad film about three animals that got lost and Grace kept greeting and Senga had had to hold it in, eyes all filling up but the sound of Grace greeting like that made it impossible. Then on the road home, they'd asked if she hadn't liked the film, just because she hadn't been greeting as well. As though she was faulty or something.

It just froze her up so she never knew what she really felt about things at all. This story about the garden wasn't even all that sad. Felix didn't look the gardening type, thin fingers like a doctor. If you really thought about it, you could see how the garden would quite annoy him, having to be looked after when it wasn't his really. Thinking about it that way made it easier. Duncan was still waiting with the empty cup.

I'll take these in, she said. Maybe I'll go and see.

Duncan smiled. He probably thought she wanted to go and moon about on her own now, thinking about the daft story. It was impossible to shake him off.

That's the girl.

She felt him watch her all the way up the path, grinning before he stuffed himself back into the waiting gullet of the car.

The trees had looked small from the window. Underneath, even the lowest bits made you reach, leaves bunched together where the fruit was thickest: green, red, purple and black color all on the same branch. Loads of things. It made her dizzy leaning back to look up but she didn't want to lean against the tree itself. There was no telling what was living in it, under the bark. She staggered backward as her foot slipped on something soft, more of them on the ground between the bits of fallen bark. Windfalls: that thick sweet smell like metal. It was fermenting. That was what happened to rotten fruit. It lay and rotted and the sugars came out and something else, she forgot what. Wanting to look closer, she dropped to her hunkers and reached for the nearest. Dark red, the skin loose and warm. It slipped when you touched, the flesh separate and firmer underneath. Her finger left a dark shape of itself where it melted off the bloom. She opened her hand and picked up the whole fruit; thumb and first fingertip, end to end, lifting it nearer. Then it became something else. Grey blue fungus furred one side of a gash underneath, a running sore oozing brown pulp and something else. Something moving. Thin black feelers twitching toward her hand. Dropping it was immediate. Even then it wasn't far enough away and she drew back from under the shade of the trees, staring, wiping her hands against the jean seams to get rid of the feel from her fingers. Black movements flickered at the corners of her eyes, everywhere now she looked. Ants. It was just ants. Ants couldn't do you any harm. The grass kept moving, wriggling under her feet. Shivering, she went inside for a cardigan.

Lunch.

At home you call it dinnertime but it is really lunch.

Cold meat and pickles, halved tomatoes, bread and butter for three. Felix was still out. Grace took a notion to sit out afterward but nobody else wanted to. Senga watched from the window as she appeared outside alone with a candy-stripe chair and a magazine. The magazine flapped too much when she tried to read it so she had to give up and just sit, staring into space. From inside, the windowframe made a border, like a painting. Whistler's mother. It waved at the girl looking out, pretending to be comfortable.

The girl spread her cards on the tablecover. Three. You had to send postcards but they were always difficult, especially when you hadn't done anything. The things on the fronts of the cards didn't help either: pictures of the model village about twenty years out of date. The wee boys in the background were wearing shorts and school caps. School caps for heaven's sake. Another one had no people: just the models pretending to be the real thing but you could tell if you looked hard: the smoothness of the road gave it away. She flipped one over.

Dear Mum, the house is lovely and the weather is nice and warm. This is the model village, we went there yesterday and it is lovely. We had our dinner out in the garden. We are having a great time. Don't miss me too much haha. Uncle Felix is asking for you.

Grace seemed to have fallen asleep. The girl watched the bird-flap of the fallen magazine, sun through the window falling hot on her neck. Twice, the slide of her elbows jerked her awake.

The third time it was the clink of bottles.

Then two voices. A man and a woman. The garden chair was empty. It was Grace in the kitchen speaking to someone. Felix. It wasn't possible to hear the words properly but you could tell who it was all right. She pushed her feet against a table spar and stretched, listening. There weren't any men at home. Duncan didn't count. It was good to listen just to the depth of it, the low echo coming through the wall, rocking on two legs of the chair with her eyes closed. It could only have been moments. Then a snap that meant someone had gotten off one of the kitchen chairs. Before the girl had time to open her eyes, Grace's voice came again, clear as though she had spoken in the same room.

She's bound to be funny, a bit withdrawn. You know what I mean. Not like a normal lassie.

There was a sound that could have been a cupboard opening.

I wouldny say anything against Greta but she's still thon bitter way. She says things, twisted things. Have the wean twisted as well before she's finished.

The voice dipped further.

See it already.

Her footing slid on the table rung as the chair tipped four-square on the carpet. They could have heard it. The girl looked round to the kitchen door. They would think she was here on purpose, listening deliberately to people who thought they were private. It was too late just to appear round the door and say: they would wonder why she had been waiting so long before coming through. It would look worse. But they were bound to come through eventually and it wouldn't be good to be here, in this place. Silently, she gathered up the cards and slid the chair under the table where it belonged. The carpet shuffled again when she moved, when she tried to inch the door back. It was nearly wide enough.

There you are.
Felix watched her from the kitchen hatch.
What are you being so quiet about then eh?
He was smiling and trying not to, amused by her. Her mouth stayed shut.
Anyway, just the girl I'm looking for. Duncan says you're asking about the garden, about the trees and things.
The girl couldn't remember. Her neck was hot.
I went for a look. Just a wee look at them. Just to see.
Maybe she had done something wrong and should apologize. Maybe he didn't like her going into the garden. June's garden. Maybe because she hadn't asked first.
It's lovely, she said. The flowers and everything.
Sometimes compliments made things better. He was scratching behind his ear, not really listening.
Said he thought you wanted to pick some fruit or something, yes?
She couldn't remember saying anything like that. Not out loud and not to Duncan because he repeated things you'd said. He anticipated: interceded without being asked. And he got things all wrong. It would be Duncan right enough then: something she'd said and he'd mixed it up as usual. Her own fault for saying anything in the first place. She

nodded to accept her part of the blame. He wasn't even looking.

Why not eh? Doing me a favor, pet, tidying the place up a bit. I'm afraid it doesn't get the attention these days. Be my guest. Unless—

He shrugged. She was trying not to think about ants and adjusted her face to look happier. It wasn't a row after all.

No, I'd like to. I would. I can even go now if you like. I can get them for teatime, put them on the table mibby. I would like to.

It came out too quick and stuttery but he looked pleased.

Whatever you like, sweetheart. Yes. Now if you want.

He squeezed her backside as she went through to the kitchen, then shouted after as she sprinted out over the grass.

Watch out for the wasps.

The thin face in one oblong of the window lattice. She kept her back to it and tilted up, ignoring the movement in the leaves, reaching with her eyes tight shut.

Duncan said they gave him heartburn and the skins got beneath his plate. But they looked nice. Everybody said they looked nice, washed and buffed in a glass dish on the table. They all ate sponge cake instead.

Always tell homemade.

Grace had icing sugar on her chin.

Get a nice one at the WI on a Tuesday. Felix sucked his fingertips and picked up crumbs. Answer to a bachelor's prayer.

Duncan didn't say anything, just belched. He always did it at the end of a meal when there was nothing else to come. Grace usually said You're welcome I'm sure but didn't to-night. It was because she hadn't made the cake. They left

the plums and went to the sofa, then Felix brought out a
bottle of whisky.

Bugger the washing up, he said.

They all laughed and he said it again.

Bugger it. Let's be wicked for once.

After a while he put a record on as well. They can't take
that away from me. Frank Sinatra. They sang bits of the
lines and all joined in on the last one. Duncan poured more
drink and put on Harry Belafonte. They weren't really listening anymore anyway. Grace was doing the story about
the time they got chased by somebody when they were
teenagers and other stuff would follow that, things about
before Senga was born. They were all meant to be funny.
Grace hooted at her back while the girl watched the needle,
the seasick bounce over and over because the record was
finished. They said nothing about her father. Maybe there
weren't any funny stories about him. The turntable started
buzzing. A chink of glasses.

Someone carried her to bed.

Shot.

A crack and patter of applause. A man in white glared as
he followed the line, shadows chasing the soles of canvas
shoes. Slingbacks weren't allowed on the grass.

Heavy.

Groans and hands up to chins. No cloud overhead. The
square of crew-cut green was open to the sky. Borders
behind the three benches had rosebushes pruned back to
stumps, acid fists that would be dahlias in a couple of
weeks but were nothing yet. A few everlasting daisies
stared dry-eyed up at the sun. The other two benches were
empty.

Wide.

The girl stretched, pulled at the neck of her shirt as Grace came back near the trench, kicking the bowls with the sides of her shoe.

Aunty Grace.

Aunty. Wee girl voice.

Can I go for a walk. A wee walk. Just the shops.

Grace's eyes were blanked out with the light on her specs.

Just a look at the shops.

Grace kept looking, her mouth slack. The girl pursed her lips. It was hard not to get fed up with it, knowing what was most likely coming anyway: all the daft questions before you got to do anything on your own. No you wouldn't get lost and yes you knew what the address was, you knew where the bus stop was and to ask if you got lost, etc. As if you were going to get lost on purpose. It would have been quicker at home. But Grace wasn't her mother. She was just being careful in case she got landed with the blame for not looking after you right. Her toes were sore, crushed into the pointy tips of these shoes. She couldn't think why she'd worn them.

Someone shouted: it was nearly Grace's turn. She came up to the side of the ditch, raking in the big cardigan pockets, the end of her tongue poking between the teeth. She found what she was looking for and reached, unsmiling, to push it into the girl's hand.

Back for your tea, mind. Don't get lost.

A key and money: a pound note wrapped round loose change. She was halfway up the green when the girl looked up, past where Felix was stooping, peering under his hat for the jack. Duncan waved.

Boots the chemist: blue and white, reliably the same. It flipped the street into something more familiar through the arcade of antiques and gothic lettering. Antiques for heaven's sake, six in the one stretch of road. She bought nail varnish. Sugar Plum: private joke. Then a cup of coffee in the tearoom with Grace's money. Outside, there wasn't much else worth seeing. It was when she crossed the road to check times from the bus stop she saw the sign to the museum. It pointed behind the place they'd bought the postcards the other day, in a square of ground with what looked like gravestones outside. There was no one on the door and inside, just a big room like a drill hall ranged with cases, a sentence dying into echo as two people at the far end turned to look. She walked to the first cases, as they turned away, keeping her shoes quiet on the wooden floorboards. Bits of flint tricking the light as fossil remains, old coins and nails. The open display of farming things was better: thatching tools and a cider press with a carved wooden bore like a giant thumbscrew. At least they looked local. Threshing things, flails, rakes with rows of blunt teeth, a scythe. At the far end of the hall, stocks, manacles and a round cage affair hung on the wall. A scold's bridle. The metal hoop had bands of rusty iron on either side and a hinged piece that forced a flat iron spike inside the mouth when it closed. Some had points to prevent the mouth from closing, others, leather tongues to soak up saliva. For wives who scolded or told lies. The card used exclamation marks to show it was a kind of joke. War memorabilia took up all the rest: child's gas mask, a ration book with unused coupons, a parish register with brown writing, pinned like butterflies on green baize. The last was a free-standing glass box under the exit sign, with an old shop dummy in RAF blue and some other bits and pieces. HEMMINGFORD UNDER FIRE. The uniform was too big so the dummy's limbs looked wasted, the painted hair and the eyes had peeled down to the plaster. Sellotaped at eye level, a smeary photograph of a man in an open field. He was holding a chunk of metal and smiling

fit to bust. ENEMY AIRCRAFT SHOT DOWN OVER LOCAL FIELD
1944.

It was over the man's shoulder now she looked again, like
a dinosaur carcass. The fuzziness in the distance could have
been smoke. The chunk of metal in his hands was identifiable at the bottom of the case. It looked blacker in the
photo but then they'd have polished it. The bits were still
stained when you looked hard, blotched with yellow and
brown where they sat on that shiny cloth. If she tilted her
head she could see a card between folds. Parachute silk,
unused. Her eyes flicked back to the photo. Cows near the
back of the field and a washing line in the distance, trees
and smoke: the burned-out shell dripping wreckage like
rotten meat. In the spaces between, unimaginable things.
The card at the dummy's feet said the parachute had never
been used. Inside the Sellotape rim, the farmer grinning out
at the camera like he was on his holidays. He had terrible
teeth.

Someone coughed. A man near the fire extinguisher, clinking keys. The couple had left already. Closing time was
5:30. It would be after that now. The girl uncurled her hand
from the coins in her pocket, the palm scored and smelling
of stale metal. She didn't even know what the fare was,
when the buses came. After promising as well. After
promising.

Grace was setting the table herself when she got back,
breathless to show she'd been running. There was no row.
Grace was in a good mood, singing when she brought
through the plates. Tongue salad. Nobody else said anything about being late either. In the end, it turned out she

wasn't: they were having tea earlier because they were going out, just the pub at the other side of the village with some people Felix knew.

You wouldny be wanting to come really eh?

Grace spoke through the last mouthful of something. Half a scone sat among the chip smears and leftover salt on her plate.

Would you eh? You could come but it's a pub. You don't like that kind of thing eh? All old folk as well.

Oldies right enough.

Duncan tapped the heel of his knife on the table, eyes on the butter.

It's an old folks' outing haha.

You can come if you want, love. Felix lifted his cup. Let her come if she wants.

It's no interesting for a lassie her age though. Bowling club talk. It's no interesting is it? You wouldny find it interesting. Do you think you would? Sure you wouldny?

It was the cartoon voice again. The girl shook her head, watching with her hand over her mouth.

See?

Felix kept his face straight. He looked like the photo of her father. Senga shook her head.

Honest. I'm not bothered.

Grace was pleased, pouring tea the girl didn't want, adding milk and sugar without asking.

Likes to read, she said. Probably quite pleased we're away, eh?

They gave her Dairy Box in a cellophane wrapper and a reminder she could come if she liked. The car dipped out of the drive with hands in every visible window, waving as though they were away for years.

The talking head on TV was still reading news, Duncan's program. She tried all the buttons then switched it off. The records were no use and there wasn't even anything worth reading: a pile of ancient *Readers' Digests* full of American things and jokes that weren't funny, drawings that didn't look like real people's insides. Half the time they did them blue or green for heaven's sake. She stacked them back into the bookcase in the right order, the newest-looking one on top. A jigsaw or something would have been good but she didn't know if he had one, where he'd keep such a thing if he did. It was still someone else's house, someone else's things. Different rules about what was what, being feart to do things in case they got on somebody's nerves. Without him here it was just the same. There was dust all over her fingers. Nobody could have touched those magazines for years. The photos on the walls were all ancient, all men and airplanes. There was nothing to do down here. She looked up at the ceiling then walked out into the hall. It was getting dark already. Those coats behind the door like hunched shoulders over big wooden pegs. It got to that in-between time of night quicker here, when it was too dark with the light not on but that horrible yellow color when it was. She put the light on anyway, showing up the stouriness of everything, ridges of it along the banister rim. It was even darker upstairs. Looking at it made her stomach feel cold. But all you had to do was refuse to look scared then nothing could touch you. And there was the switch down here as well. Stupid. Her neck prickled as she reached and put on the second switch, watching the light bleed out over the steps. Being feart like this was stupid.

A glow of streetlights filled the landing window when she got to the top, somebody whistling outside. Knowing there were people outside was a good thing, even if you couldn't see who. The nearest bedroom door was off the catch, a pair of Duncan's green socks just inside on the floor. They made this whole end of the landing smell salty. The door opposite was shut. Properly shut. It wasn't near enough the window to see much from here: a reflected row of other bedroom windows, curtains and lampshades. The whistling was fainter. The shut door seemed closer.

Hardly had to touch the handle at all.

A dark smell like ham spice curled out, thickening the air like dust. Uncle Felix's room. It would be beneath her own, the square of visible window showing the same leaves. Their shadows twitched along the facing wall to make patterns on the dresser. Even in this half-light, you could see the top had just a hairbrush and a comb, a few china figurines. None of the clutter of bottles and lotions that covered everything at home: female things. The dresser mirror filled completely with red candlewick reflection from the double bed and there was a backward photo over the headboard. She cut free from the door one finger at a time and stepped beyond the threshold, slowly in case the boards creaked. It was a wedding photo, the woman in a wedding dress, yards of net from the headdress drifting across the man's dark suit, the lipstick black inside the white face. There were more people behind them. The extra step nearer to see was too close, dunting heavily into the bedside table. The lamp rocked but stayed upright. She'd have to be more careful, reaching to straighten the shade, smooth over the cloth on the surface. It had two cigarette burns along one edge. Then beneath, inside the shelf, she saw the magazine. Huge breasts and painted nails on the cover. She held her breath, staring, then reached and picked it up. The pages were thick and dry, wavy as though it had been dropped in the bath. The woman came closer, pushing her own breasts together with those long-fingered hands. The next page was much the same, this time with the woman looking right at you, that terrible old-fashioned makeup round her eyes. Just staring, sticking out her tongue. The girl swallowed and lifted another page. This time the paper tugged back, just once before it gave, unpeeling with a light rip. The girl's stomach dipped as she opened it out to see. Tear marks: two women's faces seamed with white where the paper had separated. She shut the magazine then opened and shut it again. She turned the right page to the top before she put it back in place and walked backward out of the room, closing the door quietly, listening. There was nothing to hear except the buzz of the overhead bulb; her own heartbeat as she stood at the top of the stairs, holding her breath. That prickling feeling along the back of the neck that let you know you were being watched. Sweating now, the girl turned, clutching and unclutching her palms. A sheen of eyeless smiles, the watchers looked back. Just photographs, barrack-boy grins from the frames on the landing, their thread of soundless laughter spinning a web into the thick air, the space between herself and the way down. She shut her eyes and kept walking.

The garden was just blackness falling from a ragged line of royal blue, a super-imposed ghost of herself floating in the way. There was no telling how much longer it would be. But she wouldn't go up to bed. Not till they were back. Her stomach flexed as she poured cold tea down the sink and made a fresh cup, wandered back along the hall carrying it close to her chest. No more noises. That creaking upstairs was just beams, wood settling. That was what wood did, it settled. Creaked and groaned in the joists. She fumbled a hand round the corner into the living room to switch on the light, then walked across to the window. Nothing. The TV was still terrible. It would be good to be able to stop thinking about the magazine, about going into the upstairs room. But it wasn't possible to forget. Not possible. Not possible to say to anyone either because. Just because. She didn't want this tea either.

Halfway to the kitchen she stopped and looked to the top of the stairs again, listening, in case. The door opened too

suddenly then, thudding hard against the inside wall as Felix
stumbled in over the step then the cup was falling from her
hands, spattering tea and broken china as Grace appeared
too, stopping talking in midflow. The beer haze thickened
as they stood, looking at her clueless in the middle of what
she'd done. Outside, "Clementine" whistled on oblivious
through the shutting of car doors. Felix moved first.

Oops.

The voice was too loud.

Oops. That was silly.

It slurred. Grace was away to the kitchen for a cloth already
as he came forward, touching the girl's shoulder. She
couldn't look up, couldn't lift her eyes from the mess seeping
through the carpet pile and turning it black. Duncan's voice
saying What's up? at the door and Felix asking if she was
all right, nudging the shoulder under his hand.

You're shaking, pet. It's all right. No harm done.

She could scent drink, the slurriness in the voice. He turned
away and spoke at Duncan's face as Grace pushed through,
scrubbing with the cloth at the wet carpet.

No need to be upset eh, he said.

Grace snorted, still scouring, then cut her finger on a chip
of cup handle and said Bugger it. Bugger it. Grace hardly
ever swore. Yet the girl's mouth wouldn't open, that knot
in her throat like sickness rising till it hurt while Felix
watched. Duncan kidding on he was invisible at the door.
This fuss over nothing. Grace sucked her finger.

Silly lassie.

Struggling not to be angry. It was worse than shouting. It
was terrible, so embarrassing you wanted to faint just to
escape from it, you wanted to die. The girl's throat con-
stricted sharply. Bad to worse, that horrible greeting noise
in the middle of no noise at all and she was making it, not
able to stop. A sigh. Grace would be shaking her head.

What's the matter now eh? You tell me.

She's all right. Shhh. Just leave it be. Leave it just now.
They were supposed to be whispering. The dishcloth shifted
in Grace's hands. She was angry.
Shh. You're all right, love. Aren't you? All right, eh? No
harm done. That big hand wrapping her shoulder again.
I'll take her up maybe. Just tired. Tired eh? She's all right
now though. She's all right.

It felt terrible smiling, knowing her face would be swollen,
but it was what he wanted her to do. He waited till she'd
done it. Even remembering about the magazine, she creased
her swollen lids and smiled.

Grace was already at the sink, polishing knives.
You're early, she said.
Nothing else. She went on dropping things into the drawer.
The table was already set. The girl crossed to the window
and looked out to avoid conversation. The noise of cutlery
stopped, exchanged itself for the rustle of bread. Paint runs
over the lip of the sill came into focus, sharp white against
the haze of leaves and sky outside as Grace started singing,
rattling the grill. She was being polite on purpose but that
didn't mean she didn't remember. The smell of fat and
burning crumbs. The idea of food made her feel sick. She
wasn't wanting any breakfast. Wasn't wanting to be here,
the kitchen too full of smoke and not talking, the feeling
you weren't able to get away. Outside in the garden would
do, up at that fence and looking out over the road, watching
the cars going past. No hills, no sea; but at least the cars
going somewhere. If she could just open her mouth, open
it and ask. She sighed instead, hearing Duncan's shuffling
along the hall in his socks.
Aye aye.

Grace pouring water for tea and the creak of floorboards. There was no point in being at the window anymore. It was misted over with steam.

Aye aye.

He had on those green socks, the ones off the bedroom floor the other night. Her back straightened as she inhaled, mouth searching for a smile. Duncan came across with the pot, a handful of spoons, grinning. She watched her hands, turning cups upright in their saucers, without focusing her eyes. That way, she managed when Felix came through. She managed all the way through breakfast.

Don't run away and hide. Little piece of information.

He called her back as she left the table. He was waving a cigarette when she turned, digging the fingers of his other hand into the matchbox.

Outing. Leave about twelve or say. Time to put on a frock if you like eh? And a smile.

He looked up as the match sparked.

Pretty girl when you smile.

The glass was too full, spilling when she walked. It got worse when you concentrated, the sides getting slippy so it was getting hard to hold, the plate in the other hand not able to be put down. And so many people. The Fox and Grapes was full of horse brasses and pictures of dogs, little lamps with leatherette shades. The tables were packed close and too wee, but they crammed tight, a circle of the glasses in the middle and the plates on their knees. Pork pies and cider: Felix said they had to. They just started when two other men came and Felix rolled his eyes. His mouth was full of pie. He swallowed and said everybody's names. The men said Ock Eye the Noo and Hoots Mon then pretended they thought Senga and Grace were sisters before they went away again, kissing hands. Duncan thought they were well on. Every so often, they waved.

The pie was fatty. Senga left most of it and ate the bits of salad while the place got noisier. Felix winked at her drinking the cider and they went back in a good mood, the two men still in there at the bar, shouting Cheerio. But it was hot on the walk home and the headache the girl had been trying to ignore in the pub got worse. By the time they got back it was making her eyes hurt. When she asked to lie down, Duncan laughed. He said it was the cider. It might have been true: the stairs were making her feel worse. She ignored the clothes over the floor, the bed left unmade from the hurry this morning and crossed to the window, pressing her forehead at the cool, flat glass. It was good momentarily but heated up too fast and left marks when she pulled away. Outside, wet leaves splayed flat between drips of condensation. Fresh. They made you want to reach out, reach your whole self in among them with your eyes shut, touching till your clothes stuck to the skin. The idea of cool leaves on your eyelids, the soreness inside the head. Closing her eyes made her dizzy and she opened them again. At least she could open the window. It looked as if it hadn't been opened for years, paint along the inside of the catch. It was stiff even when she pushed with both hands. On the next push it gave, cracking as the frame breathed out. It didn't open far because the hinge was painted too, but already bits of twig poked into the space she made, widening the air inside the room with nervous momentum, the smell of green. It opened out inside your lungs when you breathed. She flexed her fingers and slid her arm outside. Touching one leaf made the rest dip, balancing drops of water, drumming when they fell. Lower down, the plums made soft thuds against the glass. She could reach from here, if she stretched, stood on her toes. It was easier if she turned her head to the side, then she could feel them just within and out of reach, tipping the backs of her fingernails. She relaxed her shoulder then held her breath to stretch again, pressing her side against the window. Something touched back this time: a sizzle on the skin that made her draw back suddenly, scattering water as far as the quilt.

It didn't hurt immediately.
The incision, though certainly felt, was not pain. More like burning: the root of her index and middle fingers with these tiny pinholes when she looked. Stings. That was what it had to be though she had never been stung before. It was different to what you thought: not sore to start with. But hoping it would go away wasn't going to work. She could feel it already as she tried to close the window again, pushing out stray ends of tree. When she looked again it was swollen, filling out with heat. It even looked different, curled like a claw on the end of her wrist. Her own fault: she shouldn't have been opening the window in the first place and now she'd have to go down and tell them, make another fuss after last night. But she'd have to: this searing getting worse. As long as there wasn't any more of that crying, not this time. The important thing was not to cry.

White as a sheet, love.
She wished it hadn't been Felix but it was. Felix who was there at the foot of the stairs, who took her along the hall to a cupboard under the stairs smelling of must and turps, reached under the sink for a plain bottle, then slackened the top with one hand with the other tightening on the wrist as though he were trying to cut through to the bone. It hurt. Everything had hurt, like when he pushed her hand into the brown puddle at the bottom of the sink and held it there but she hadn't given anything away. His grip slack-

ened as the throbbing died down. Now it was almost soothing, just a pulse under the skin. There was sweat through
the smell of vinegar and she noticed how close they were.

White as a sheet.

The sink made a noise as it drained. The man stood back,
reaching for a crumpled tube on the surround.

Nasty. How'd you manage that one?

Looking out the window, she said. They must have been
on the ledge, something like that.

The words were shaky and not easy to control. She knew
she was going to lie.

It was when I was tidying, putting things away.

She didn't know why she was saying these things. Her
mother said she couldn't tell the truth about anything, never
admitted to anything.

I just didn't see them.

The stink of vinegar and the heat in the tight space was
making her dizzy. He patted her hair and drew her nearer
his chest, tipping her forehead with his lips.

There, pet. Too easily upset, you know. It doesn't matter.

She was blushing now, knowing he was thinking about last
night. Her stomach dipped. Maybe he had found the magazine.

Spilt milk and all that. Life isn't as serious as you think.

His heartbeat, the ridge of his vest under her cheek, the
smell of hothouse. Nothing else. She pulled away and smiled
because it was what he wanted. That way he might leave
her alone.

That's my girl, that's more like it.

She nodded to let him know that's just what she was. Just
his girl.

They sat her outside all afternoon, dosing her with cups of
sickly tea and Grace's magazines. Felix was drying dishes
when she came back in. He heard her coming and wiped

his hands. They'd eaten, he said: thought she'd fallen asleep and hadn't wanted to wake her up after all that excitement. There were sandwiches left on the table, covered; a slice of cake. Duncan and Grace were out. The girl pushed her plate to the edge of the table, her back to him.

Aren't you going as well?

She was lifting and laying the knife, studying the blunt edge.

I mean how come you're not going out too?

The whisper of drying cloth stopped.

You don't have to. You don't need to if it's because, it's just me. I'm all right.

He started the drying again.

I know.

There was a dry click as he sat something on the surface. Now, will I put on tea or not?

She nodded and lifted one of the sandwiches. Triangles.

How's the hand?

A shout through the noise of filling kettle.

She looked down, gripped her fingers with her mouth full of fish paste. Now he asked, it was stiff. And reeking of vinegar.

They spent the evening watching the end of a film, the news, then a serial that meant it was Thursday, making jokey remarks about the programs: silences between. Her mother didn't like talking with the TV on. Shhhhh all the time. Shhh to hear the words. It occurred to the girl she was happy. He liked her being there. Maybe she would be able to get round to the subject of her father. Dad. The word never felt right. What she could remember wasn't good: cigarette burns, the stink of drink and being woken up in the dark, shouting. Crying and hysterics. A man propped up against hospital pillows not sure who she was. She sang to him and he cried before Grace took her away. She didn't even know what it was he'd died of. Maybe that would make a difference. But this wasn't the right time: it would spoil things. They ate the last of the chocolates, cherry cup and orange cream. They tasted of vinegar. Felix said he could smell her from here and ran her a bath, shouting up the stairs while she undressed. Maybe he even liked her. But he hadn't found the magazine. Not yet.

A single-bar heater was burning in the attic when she came back from the bath, the curtains drawn. And a dressing gown behind the door, pink with shiny cuffs and shoulders. Grace was right enough: he spoiled folk. The dressing gown was too nice to put on, that cold feel from the satin, a scent of stale powder. She put it back on the hook and dropped the towel, walking toward the fire. She could see herself in the mirror now, skin scarlet from the orange glow, red buttons on her chest, a heart shape of hair where the legs stopped. The face wasted it. She turned away from the mirror and stooped for the switch on the side of the fire. The wrong hand. She pulled it back too late: heat had already drawn the stings to a pulse again. It kept her restless all night.

Here's Sleeping Beauty, here she is.
Grace snapped the girl's bra strap as she went past.
Dozy Dora. Rascal.
Duncan was much the same.
Did you forget eh? Last day of the holidays and you forget? I don't know. What'll we do with ye?

The smell of fish and coffee hung over the kitchen. Felix brought a bottle of milk and examined her hand before he went back to the window, not joining in. He sometimes ate standing there as well. Grace sat toast on the girl's plate and nudged the butter across. They'd had a good night out, folk they hadn't seen for ages. Now it was her turn. They could go into town for a look at the market stalls if she liked.

Wee look round, said Grace. Souvenirs. You like that kind of thing.

Duncan scratched his nose with the end of the buttery knife.

And photos. Canny go home without the photos. Sure ye can't? Show your mum the good time you've been having.

Felix poured what was left of his tea down the sink.

Well then. Five minutes girls.

The toast was cold. Even with butter on, it wouldn't be nice. The girl settled for tea as Duncan got up to take Felix's place at the window, looking out. The sky was thick blue. Aye aye he said and sighed. Grace started stacking plates.

Yoohoo.

Duncan took a picture of Felix looking up. Grace wasn't pleased. That wouldn't look like anything, he wasn't doing the thing right at all. She stood beside the car, coat over her arm, waiting till they lined up. He took two beside the car before she shifted them again. Two next to the flower border before Duncan took over. They moved round the side of the house, in front of the trees, into the back porch, near the ivy up the side wall then back again for some in the drive. There were some under the window from a distance to show the thatch and the grass before Grace took a crabbit turn and refused to stand in the sun anymore. Felix posed at his front door alone, then for another with his arm round Senga. He took the camera himself for the last one, of Duncan, standing to attention at the car. The plastic seats were sticky and too hot when they got in.

That's what you get for bringing it out of the shade, Grace said.

Her lipstick was starting to melt.

She blamed the crowds on Duncan as well.

Supposed to get here early and avoid this. Photos.

He wasn't bothered, just went off on his own to a stall with car sponges and windscreen wipers. Grace said he would probably stand there all day. The others stayed together and looked at tea towels, butter dishes, key rings. Lunch was bacon-and-egg pie from a stall with coffee in waxy cups. They decided to walk back for the fresh air so they didn't have to get in the car: it had been parked out of the shade again. Duncan would need to drive it back himself. He finally took the huff.

It'll not be this tomorrow, he said. Not be much walking back home. I bet it's raining in Saltcoats.

Och Duncan, said Grace with her mouth twisted. Last day for goodness' sake. Sicken your happiness. Just be quiet if you canny say something nice. Just give us all peace.

She kept going even after he'd left, silent and with his jaw tight.

Ye can't have everything. After all we've got the scenery. The mountains and the scenery.

There was a pause as if she had forgotten the next sentence before she repeated herself.

The mountains and the scenery after all.

The mountains. There weren't any mountains in Saltcoats. Just the shore and the smell of rotten seaweed. The mountains were in the Highlands and they had never been there. But Duncan shouldn't have upset her like that. It was too soon to think about tomorrow but now he had forced it on them. The journey north, stuck in the car for hours at a strict fifty while other cars overtook: sandwiches and tea from a flask, stuffiness and stops at petrol stations for toilets with queues and no paper. Last day as well. He shouldn't have. But he had now. Grace was upset. It kept up through the afternoon, the ferrying back and forth to the bedroom, packing and changing her mind about things, muttering. The best thing to do was keep out of her road, out of Duncan's road too while he footered with the engine, the same as usual, staring under the bonnet and polishing things that were already clean. At the back of the house there was only flat distance beyond the trees, quiet. Felix was standing looking out over the fence. It just reached the level of his eyes. He knew she was there without turning round.

Just thinking the place needs attention eh? I never seem to have time. Anyway. He clapped his hands and rubbed them together. All packed up for the off?

They looked at each other and his smile got wider.

Been a quick week. You can get too used to your own company.

A wasp hovered silently near his shoulder, then shifted toward the fence slats. He caught the line of her eye and turned to see.

Past their best.

She couldn't think.

Keep meaning to thin them. Know who liked those?

The sweet peas; he thought she was looking at the sweet peas.

Your dad, love. He liked all the colors.

He put his hands in his pockets and straightened.

Just a tiny little thing the last time I saw you, just so high. He estimated off the ground with one hand. And look at you. Makeup and nylons. You wonder where the time goes. You remember your dad?

He cleared his throat.

You can ask about him if you like.

They looked at the grass, the tip of his shoe pawing a channel. The girl's chest felt tight and she didn't know what to say. Photos weren't it: they had photos at home. And that wasn't really like knowing anybody. But this stuff about what flowers he liked or the color of his hair wasn't it either. You couldn't ask what was he like: that was the kind of question you never got much of an answer for. Or it got turned into something else: drunk and violent, a good thing he died when he did, wasted his life and tried to waste everybody else's etc., etc. Her mother did all that stuff without asking and it still told you nothing. So what was it? She looked at the man's shoelaces while he waited, not knowing. If she didn't speak soon, he'd get fed up or talk about something else, walk back to the house and that would be it finished. She'd never get the chance again.

A cigarette slid between the thin lips when she looked up, the hand reaching for it smooth and clean. He had them manicured, Grace said. Manicured. All that Englishness and the house and the smoothness of everything about him. He had no children. The idea made her suddenly angry, furious. The match flared, the soft hand cupping the flame. He had no children. But that was a terrible thing to say to anybody, blame them for not being your father. It didn't even make sense. The spent match fell and sizzled momentarily on the damp grass. She knew she was blushing. When he started to move away, his profile fading through the trail of smoke; when it was that split second over the edge of too late; then, she knew. She knew what she should have asked all along. What was *his spit*? This thing she was, just his spit? And forming the question, she suddenly suspected the answer. It was something too terrible to know about, something nobody would say to you even if you asked, even if they understood. She watched his back, the smoke drift toward her from somewhere in front of where he was and knew she would not say, she could not say that question. It was the only question but not possible to ask. She could not speak.

Felix scratched his ear.

Getting maudlin in my old age. I just wanted to know if you were happy. You are happy, aren't you? Does it make you happy being here, love?

She opened her mouth, hoping, but nothing came out. He stroked her hair then moved under the trees. She knew when he spoke his voice would be changed.

Ought to do something about these too.

Her eyes prickled.

All this bloody fruit. Ought to pick some of it. Waste otherwise.

Yes, she said, a long sigh. It was her own fault. The moment was gone now anyway.

What do you say?

She said nothing.

Pick some of this? We could manage just the two of us.

He was talking about the plums, making an offer. It was ungrateful to keep him waiting like this, as though she didn't care. She tried to look as though she cared.

I'll get something to put them in if you like.

Maybe, she said.

The sound of her own voice a surprise. He looked and waited.

Maybe what? Not scared after yesterday, eh?

No. Just maybe. Maybe it's a good idea.

She didn't know what it was supposed to mean either. The butt-end of the cigarette wormed on the grass under his shoe and he breathed out the last of the smoke.

Too much bother getting the ladder. We'll just see what we can reach eh? Just us two. Bugger ladders.

And he laughed, his teeth yellow under the shadow of the trees.

. . .

Chips and eggs, bread and butter, jam, chocolate biscuits. Grace was still unpredictable so they kept the noise of the cutlery low. There wasn't much chance of playing the records or TV or anything. She'd put the nail varnish on too and nobody had noticed, Duncan starting already with his road maps and muttering motorways. She and Grace tidied up silently while the men moved to the sofa, talking routes and place names. After the table was cleared, Grace looked at her watch and yawned. Eight o'clock already. She wouldn't be surprised if everyone else was tired too. She wouldn't be surprised if they would be going to bed soon. There was still packing to do after all. Senga got the one game of rummy before the cards needed to be packed up as well. The men were still playing with maps as the girl shut the door.

Beams through the ceiling. Worn red carpet and cream edging on the wood. Glass-eyed photos. She knew while she tried to absorb the details for the last time it didn't matter: what she would have to say about the house tomorrow would not be enough or not the right things. She never noticed the right things. The photograph halfway up the stairs, for example. 1944, RAF Bisley; the twelve young men still looking foreign and smiling at nothing. Stupid uniforms, the war. A lot of men talking about planes and guns, things that had nothing to do with anything. Nothing important. *They're all the same, football and fighting and drink. Motorcars. Wee boys. Bloody men.* Then she was embarrassed, alone on the stairs and embarrassed as if somebody had heard it out loud. Her mother didn't know everything. Maybe a lot of men were like that but not Felix; opening doors and helping you in and out of the car. He washed the dishes and did shopping, gave you chocolates and ran the bath, called you pet, sweetheart, love. Grey faces behind the glass, tilted hats and blobs for eyes. 1944. A lot of them would be dead by now. She hurt her eyes trying to see a resemblance to someone she knew. They say you get tearful when you're tired. Tired and overwrought. High-strung. Laughter echoed from the living room as she went on up.

The mascara no one had noticed washed down the basin after the toothpaste, spit and soap. The lilac nails would have to wait. She rinsed her mouth again and went up to her room. Bottles and bits of makeup from the dresser, cards and presents from the market, creased clothes, books, the things she stood in. No point being neat: they'd all go straight in the machine when she got back. Another reason for moaning. At least it was your own place; you had a right to be there. And it would be all right leaving, as long as they didn't have to hang around a lot with the goodbyes at the door, all that hugs and kisses stuff. It wasn't comfortable. They never did it any other time and it always made Duncan's face swell up. It would be good if they got up early, just off and away. She closed the case and the curtains then sat on the edge of the mattress. The photo of herself at the bedside said SENGA, JOCK'S GIRL. Jock's girl. Her mother never even said his name. Just your father; just his spit, his bloody spit. The nightie was packed away as well. Just like the thing, undoing clasps and raking through stuff that was already away. The nightie was no great shakes either: terrible state. She kicked the case aside again, reaching her arms up to put it on. The cloth tumbled over her bare legs, the hem swaying to her knees. Then a noise like wood cracking, somewhere close. She straightened the sleeves, listening.

Only me, pet.

The handle turning so the shadow of the door inched across the rug.

Are you decent?

She looped the loose shred of lace fraying off the sleeve inside her hand just in time.

All right eh? as he came inside, round-shouldered, as if the ceiling was too low. All right? Didn't get much of a chat tonight, did we?

She smiled.

Nice holiday, pet?

Yes, lovely. It was lovely.

The nightie felt too short, dingy. He would know it hadn't been washed all week because they hadn't done any washing. He coughed and moved a step nearer.

Got something for you. That's why I came up just now. Going to give it to you tomorrow but, one thing and another.

A slim red case, held out as an invitation to look, not to speak but to look.

Something I hope you'll have.

She was going to have to take this thing, open her hand and take it. He would see the cuff, that tatty lace.

Thinking how I'd never given you anything before, nothing particular. Never got round to coming up when you were smaller, didn't see you as much as I maybe should have eh? You or your mum.

He slid a fingernail along the gold rim of the lid, prizing it up.

There. Doesn't make up for lost time, but it's yours anyway.

A string of beads on faded red velvet.

Your aunt June's, long time ago. Pearls, love. Just seed, but pearls all right.

She could feel the look through the top of her head. Her toenails were purple, glossy with varnish. Common. Sweat beaded under her arm.

Don't have to say anything, pet. Just take them. Take them for me, offering the box across. She couldn't lift her hand to take it.

To remember this old man by eh?

He was standing too close. Knowing she wasn't able for

this, that she didn't know what to say; grating the fragment
of nylon against her palm because she wasn't able to do
anything else.
Lovely. They're lovely.
The pearls lay on, misshapen in the low light. Terrifying.
They're lovely.
The box between them, too much that refused to go away.
She couldn't even thank him properly, her nails sinking into
the skin of her palm, the other hand that refused to take.
Terrible. It would be terrible if she cried. Eventually, the
box retracted. He settled it over on the bedside table, still
open.
Well.
That dullness in the voice. She knew she had disappointed
him.
Get you to bed, then. Big day tomorrow.

If there hadn't been the need to hide the painted nails, holding down her nightie with the one fisted hand. Things sticking in her throat she would never say. She could see the
photograph of herself through the crook of his arm, squint-
ing up into a black-and-white sun as he leaned to smooth
the top sheet over her chest.
Night, pet.
All she had to do was say Thank you, touch him. Sheets
tugging where his hand sunk into the mattress at her side,
warmth seeping through to the hip. He leaned to kiss her
forehead, a haze of wine and smoke from his mouth, then
back again, sitting and looking.
Sleep tight.
Sleep tight.
The skin of his cheek magnified, the depth of creases and
thread veins, unavoidable eyeballs coated with pale yellow
film. And she realized he had meant what he said, asking
her to remember this old man. And he was, he was an old

man. Pictures of him at home were turning brown. Her father's brother. She might never see him again.

Don't cry, love. Don't.

his lips parting as the breath slid out.

Cry.

Slipping.

She was reaching out to him when something started slipping. Not the covers but a hand, his hand moving closer and beneath the quilt. He was looking down into her face and touching her through the nightie while her body locked, knowing and not knowing at the same time, letting the hand search over the chest to cup one breast.

Give your uncle a kiss. Goodnight kiss.

Goodnight kiss hissing like escaping gas. The cotton slid on her legs and the headboard rocked as he pulled closer, dipping the bed with shifting weight, the dry fingers on her skin. She knew she wouldn't shout. No matter what happened she wouldn't shout. The headboard tipped the wall. Sudden and hard, the noise pulled the room too close, too real. The hand stopped, rested on her thigh through the cloth. Single strokes of the bedside clock getting louder. Then his voice, overhead.

It's all right, everything's all right, pet.

Almost a different voice. The quilt relaxed as he sighed.

You know, I used to take photos of you to work and show the boys. Wouldn't believe I had a niece so pretty, your age. Surprise, you coming so late. Your dad said you were a mistake. Mistake. But just fun, just fun. You could have made the difference to our Jock. Just like him. But you know the really telling thing is the eyes. Never heard our Grace say it but your eyes are just your mum. Just Greta looking at you. Haven't seen your mum for too long, years and years. Could have had a good life, your mum. But kept too much to herself. Too proud to ask for help, wouldn't take it. Too bloody deep. I had a soft spot for your mum.

Best legs in Scotland. And you're going to be just like her. Wanton little thing.

He lifted the hand from her nightie. She closed her eyes, not able to breathe. Something tipped her shoulder.

Pretty as a picture eh?

He waited for a moment then took his hand away altogether.

Shhh. There there. All right. I don't mean anything.

She couldn't turn, couldn't speak.

Everything's all right.

The bed creaked and rocked as he stood up. He bent for a kiss and changed his mind, hovering while she turned away, ashamed. The sudden wallpaper and its smeary roses, her lungs quiet and sore. A ghost where his hand had been on her breast.

Shouldn't take things to heart, love. Mistake.

The door clicked open. He put out the light and waited a moment in the soft grey filtering from the hall before he spoke.

Goodnight, sweetheart. Sleep tight.

The strip of gritty lace torn inside her hand.

There was the shouting from downstairs, two or three times. Finally, the footsteps. Grace, a word retracting inside the woman's open mouth.

Is the case ready? Is it?

She moved a step closer. The lipstick was too thick.

Oh dear, she said. Deary dear. I thought you weren't ready and here you are, ready all the time. Sad. That's what's the matter eh? You can always come back and see Uncle

again, back another time. Got folk worried. Just a wee bit
sad eh? Come on then. Up you pop.
She clapped her hands against her knees and went to pick
up the case, backtracking for something on the table. The
velvet box.

Look what you nearly forgot. Silly Billy. Your good
present.
The girl didn't look round.

Come on. Your uncle Duncan's waiting.
She lifted the case.

Come on.
She reached for the girl's hand and it was easy then. Wanting
to move away from this woman and her toad-skin touch.
Too fast. Her reach for the box was clumsy and the box
lid, still open from last night, snapped shut. Three or four
beads pattered onto the rug, pinholes staring up like tiny
eyes. Grace swooped right away.

For christsake lassie. Never do anything without a song
and dance. Look, you see to that and I'll take this away
down. Two minutes eh? She slotted the single pearls inside
the red box then smoothed back her hair.

Two minutes.
A watery smile.

And not have me come back up, eh?

The box shut on the bedside cabinet, the vanity case beside
the bed.

The car ticked over, getting louder as she walked down and
past the glass frames. Felix was looking up now, growing
taller till he was head and shoulders above herself and blocking the way. She could not meet his eyes. Grace's stage
whisper behind her back: Wee bit upset. He reached and
brushed his old man lips to her cheek and she tried hard to
smile. Duncan was waiting at the door with the camera. He

took a picture of the three of them coming out, heavy with cases. There were only four shots left and he wanted to finish the film.

One with Grace and her brother, cheek to cheek.
Senga and Grace stiff as toy soldiers at the front door.
Felix and his niece, arm in arm.
Then another, waving at the lens.
They grinned wider with every click of the shutter.

More kissing. The gravel under her shoes. She walked down the drive, her lungs filling as though they would never stop. Duncan took the vanity case. She watched him clear space in the boot, pushing aside two boxes of plums. A present. There was open blue above the trees and the square of green. Grace came, waving backward as she pushed inside the car, then they were all waving, the car tilting down the drive. Leaves scraped along the side windows as the carcass bounced off the pavement onto the road. As the car swung straight, a floury face appeared over the top of the bushes, blotted of features. The girl kept her head up, trying to see his eyes and waving because she was going home. Her other hand felt stiff round the narrow box in her pocket, clutched tight in case it should open and she missed the last sight of him. Grace was sighing and rummaging for maps. Duncan started whistling "Clementine" as the stink of plums began rising from the boot, thickening behind sealed windows. It went on rising all the way north.

ABOUT THE AUTHOR

JANICE GALLOWAY was born in Ayrshire, where she taught for ten years. She now makes her living as a writer and a music critic. Her adaptation of Radclyffe Hall's *The Well of Loneliness* was performed at Edinburgh's Theatre Workshop, and her first novel, *The Trick Is to Keep Breathing* (1990), won the MIND/Allan Lane Book Award, a Scottish Arts Council Book Award and was shortlisted for the Whitbread First Novel Award and the Scottish First Book of the Year. In 1991, she won the *Cosmopolitan*/Perrier Award for the best short story. She likes cities and lives in Glasgow.